SOLITAIRE

SOLITAIRE
Published by Adam Rei Books
Copyright © Barbara Lewis, 2021

ISBN: 978-1-911047-31-5

Designed by Monica Franco
www.printtailors.com

SOLITAIRE

Barbara Lewis

ADAM REI BOOKS

1

Bénédicte feels cursed not blessed. Seen from the outside, she is lucky. She could be trapped in a tiny city flat or worse. Her prison is a flint cottage with antique furniture and original art on the walls and views to die for. It is situated in a village just outside the market town of Darking, which is twinned with similarly pleasant French and German towns, except the twinning is more academic than usual, the Continent is suddenly as out of reach as if they were at war with it and there is no question of any markets taking place. Bénédicte has managed to find herself out-manoeuvred by Paul and instead of being trapped with her broken, adorable, gentle parents in the equally gentle Charente region of southwest France, he has contrived to get his wife and daughter stuck at the top of a hill in uptight Surrey with his mother, the singular Mrs Rowena Gray. Bénédicte should have guessed. If she'd followed the news more attentively, the clues were there in the fog of misinformation and government panic. Paul had interpreted them as instinctively and ruthlessly as if he were building up a trading position, carefully hedged because his native country has got itself on the wrong side of rationality, and he has bustled Bénédicte, with their teenage daughter Dominique, into the car and driven to England while it was still possible to leave and just before it became impossible to return.

"Well, here we all are," states Rowena, as they sit down to the kind of food she considers they should be eating – a daunting amount of roast chicken and over-cooked vegetables.

It seems to Bénédicte the only possible response to what she interprets as a declaration of triumph is "yes," but after a pregnant pause, Paul comes up with "and here we shall stay".

It's as if he is delivering an unpalatable truth with deafening finality. Bénédicte feels the need to soften the situation.

"I thought you were pleased," she says, resisting the temptation to switch to French.

"I am. It's just all so strange."

"It's an ill wind," says his mother.

"What do you mean, *grand-mère*?" asks Dominique, sparing Bénédicte, who is still trying to work out whether she is processing an instance of double-edged Rowena-speak or one of the many idioms she should know after a baker's dozen of years married to an Englishman.

"It's an ill wind that blows nobody any good. It's an English saying. It has the same meaning as every cloud has a silver lining. We like our metaphors," explains *grand-mère*, as Dominique calls her.

"She means that even a plague has an upside," says Paul. "Mother gets to see her grandchild."

"Could I have the pepper please?" asks Bénédicte, satisfied that this strain of conversation is, or should be, exhausted and desperate to add flavour to her pile of spring greens.

Paul nudges the grinder towards her and kicks her gently under the table. He wants her to compliment his mother on her cooking, but she isn't enough of a hypocrite. In any case, she is too busy silently wondering how many evenings are stretched ahead of her, sitting at this table without appetite, listening to Rowena comforting herself in her own opinion, as Bénédicte thinks to herself in Franglais.

She takes in the surroundings. It's one of those moments, on the surface unmomentous, but that, in the spirit of Freud, encapsulates the emotional past, present and future. Bénédicte apprehends this will be her context for weeks to come and that this evening is the model for countless others. She knows she must stifle the sense of suffocation; that everything is crowded in. She's now in a small island country, full of little Englanders for whom this quintessential cottage is a highly desirable chunk of real estate and the sprawl of her parents' home, with its over-sized pieces of French country furniture scattered casually around spacious rooms is almost unimaginable. Here nothing is casual. Everything has been carefully placed, or curated, to employ a word in its fashionable sense. There is a dresser, which Rowena has told her so many times was her mother's and is a piece of furniture she deems essential to any home. There is a grandmother clock marking every second of the time-warp they're in because a grandfather clock would be too tall and there are hand-painted scenes of the Surrey hills, that Bénédicte can see are the work of a genuine artist who had studied, felt, understood and shared with others the particular atmosphere of a particular place. She thinks Paul's father must have chosen them but doesn't raise the issue for fear it could trigger an outpouring of widow's grief and because she has an idea the English consider it bad manners to talk about the paintings on the wall over dinner.

"What's for dessert, *grand-mère*?" asks Dominique, doing her best to disguise with a carefully-positioned serviette that she has not cleared her plate. At thirteen, Dominique veers without warning between the startingly grown-up and the child-like. She's at once the indulged only grand-daughter and the solitary only child, used to adult company and conversation, but not too sophisticated to admit that the desserts of *grand-mère* tend to outshine the main course. She isn't disappointed. It's lemon meringue pie, as enjoyed by Paul throughout his childhood and to this day, but politely declined by Bénédicte, who has no taste for dessert of any kind. Rowena offers her a rather English plate of cheese. She dismisses Bénédicte's eating preferences as an affectation.

As soon as she deems it polite, Bénédicte excuses herself. She says she must call her parents and the evening is mild enough to venture outside. There is just enough light in the sky to see the shape of Box Hill and the brooding outlines of trees. She can't work out whether the silhouette, rounded and modest and concealing more than it reveals, looks so English because she knows it is. She can imagine her mother, staring out at her rose beds, as she picks up the phone to her only surviving daughter, stolen from her by a plausible English man.

2

Paul's all-time friend and sometime trading partner Bart happens to live barely a mile away in a house Rowena Gray considers vulgar with a noisy, polluting sports car sitting in the drive, and he is cooped up with his fifteen and twelve year-old daughters and a wife whose sense of happiness and self-worth until now has been based on socialising with the parents of their daughters' friends. Already, he is desperate to roar off anywhere and leave Agnieszka to argue about screen-time versus homework with Poppy and Daisy, names that Bart did not sanction. He just couldn't be bothered to argue with his strong-willed wife, who said she couldn't give them the curse of a complicated Polish name like hers. Poppy and Daisy are names she considers as the height of English fashionableness, something Bénédicte, surrounded as she is by chintz, would view as a contradiction in terms, although she understands the burden of an old-fashioned foreign name and she knows fashion must never be confused with style.

The furthest Bart dares to venture is to a bench tucked away in a nearby lane with a view of Darking and the Downs undulating all around. A brass plate affixed by his widow declares it was the favourite spot of Bert Drew, 1914-1982. Unnerved by the similarity to his own name, or at least the name he goes by, Bart ponders that Bert, whoever he was, had survived infancy during the so-called Spanish flu and presumably service in World War II. He is not convinced his floral daughters have the grit to survive another week of deprivation of the freedoms they have taken for granted, or is he just projecting? It's in fact he who can't bear the thought of not being able to do whatever he wants whenever he wants because of a risk no trader can adequately hedge of being mown down by this strange new virus that, on a whim, can leave you unscathed or gasping for breath. Even if you escape without the slightest symptom, you could pass it on to someone you love and everything that was once thoughtless fun is potentially lethal. After centuries of trial runs, the natural world has perfected its master plan to thwart decadent capitalism and avenge most subtly the wrongs boorishly inflicted by humankind.

Bart takes out his phone, modern man's preferred weapon. The obvious person to call is Paul, who, he assumes, must be as frustrated as he is. Paul for once is feeling too much else for the default boredom and frustration to have kicked in. He is clearing the table, a task that used to be performed by his father, who has been spared this unhappy phase of human history because he died five years ago of a cancer that modern medicine was powerless to halt. His mother has borne the loss with a characteristic keeping up of appearances. To the outside world she is still a robust fighter, called upon to throw herself into local issues. In her community of proud cottage gardeners and mothers whose careers have been their children and their well-managed homes, she has attracted little sympathy or concern because, consciously or unconsciously, everyone felt sorrier for him – the quiet, academic husband who followed her around, never directly challenging his domineering wife. His only obvious rebellion was to repeat her more unhinged statements out of her earshot, but just about audible as a satirical commentary for anyone who cared to tune in. Paul enjoyed the conspiratorial asides when he was around, which he now knows was never enough. He had shied away from his father in the knowledge he didn't live up to his exquisite standards. Together with so much else he has avoided examining, he never articulated it, but he believes neither of them wanted a confrontation. He has less to fear from his tougher mother and besides, he needs to make up for all those absences. Bénédicte, he tells himself, has had years with her parents. He knows he promised to commit to Cognac, but she'll just have to put up with a few weeks on his terms. His self-justification is interrupted by the welcome intrusion of his ringing phone.

"Bart!" he exclaims, heading from the room and out into the garden where Bénédicte has just finished consoling her mother that she won't see her for a while. It was a conversation infused with tearful tenderness at least on Bénédicte's side. Bart and Paul are all male bluster that gives almost nothing away. "How're you doing, mate?" "This is all a bit bizarre. Still, sure we'll be back to normal before too long." But meanwhile, they need a plan. "We could meet for a cheeky beer," suggests Bart. "Everywhere's closed," says Paul. "But we could just be going for our daily exercise and happen to meet." "And happen to be carrying beer?" "Well, you never know when you might need a drink." "When are you suggesting?" "In an hour." "Tomorrow might be easier. I'll text you."

Paul pockets his phone and ventures back into the home where he grew up and has returned in times he had never imagined living through. Had he stuck with his early idealism and become a doctor, he'd be a purposeful hero on the frontline, like Dr Rieux in *La Peste*, a work with which he is familiar from a plot summary when he was cramming at school. He left the effort of reading novels to his father. Already positioned for a life of cutting corners and taking chances, he had no patience for slow, verbal exploration or process rather than conclusion. Wondering which stocks to short and whether it is wise to meet up with the friend who somehow brings out the worst in him even in non-contagious times is so far the closest he has got to a worthwhile contribution to society.

3

Bénédicte's mother Claudine Rivet is watching *Le Cercle Rouge*. It is the first time in years she has sat down to watch any film, let alone a cult film. Her guilt is all the greater because it's the middle of the day and she had to persevere to overcome the sense of duty that decrees she should be bustling about. She was almost defeated by her unfamiliarity with their DVD player, probably last used by Bénédicte, or even Dominique, not the thirteen year-old Dominique, but Dominique, Bénédicte's late sister, killed in a horse-riding accident.

Claudine's first viewing of Melville's tense, self-consciously stylish heist drama dates back still further to a date with Jean whom she was about to marry. She tried to convince herself Jean looked like the matinee idol Alain Delon, while Jean tried to convince her he was just as cool. Those were the days when they could easily retreat into a world of make-believe because possibilities still seemed endless and they hardly knew what was true or false. Fifty years wiser, Claudine sees the ridiculous element in those flashy good looks and prefers the familiar, weather-beaten face of Jean, authentic in his quiet pursuit of his own private code.

She'd found a remastered copy of the film when she had started to tackle some of the family's decades of accumulated junk, the human-world equivalent of barnacles, which take a great deal of effort to remove. She's unsure why it's there. She knows it is critically acclaimed. She has heard people are passionate about Melville, but she has never understood why. Maybe she had talked about the film, which she remembers more for its atmosphere than for its twisting plot and Melville's made up Red Circle, non-random maxim that certain people are destined to meet, or fail to avoid each other. Indeed, their *raison d'être* is to be part of a ring of pursuers, who will inevitably shed blood. Incapable of seeking any other way to earn a living, they strain for adventure; a ring of compulsive criminals, they cannot break the vicious circle. Maybe one of her daughters had bought it out of curiosity. She can't believe Jean would have brought into the house. As far as she can tell, he'd been as baffled as she was by Melville. She's re-watching it, she tells herself, to decide whether to keep it. She doesn't explore her deeper wish to escape to a different time and reality before any of the pain of being caught up in a real-life crime drama never convincingly solved, but which she blames for the loss of her younger daughter. Without question, it also led to her losing Bénédicte to an Englishman she has always suspected of being far from innocent and who has spirited her remaining daughter away to his territory and a rival grandmother just as this new crisis has broken.

As the perfectly-judged, melancholic, slightly abrasive soundtrack begins to play, Claudine Rivet settles into a settee that probably dates from Melville's time, a time when Claudine might in forgetful moments delude herself she was happy. She knows she wasn't. Then she was racked with desire for a happy future that she now sees as earnest yet naïve, just as Melville's painstakingly constructed scenes no longer seem to her fully adult and his criminals more amateur than professional. Claudine would never have dared to persuade other people to pay for them to be played out or to watch them. Her defining youthful characteristic was the fear she would fail to achieve any kind of fulfilment and it was either self-fulfilling or prescient. Happiness has always been out of reach, like a tantalisingly close shore as she flounders in longing and heartbreak.

Jean, her rock, is lost in his world of tending vines, the structure that has supported his life. In the absence of a son, he yielded to Bénédicte's wish Paul should learn viticulture, but it was a hopeless quest. Paul showed no desire to be absorbed in the rhythm of the changing seasons and a patient response to them. His retreat is the City and its compulsion to make money quickly and defiantly; to gamble against the odds for quick losses or quick returns, not miraculous harvests and sudden blights.

Their one moment of true contact and distance has been a clash over pesticides. In what Paul regards as inconsistency, Jean relies on them to improve the yield. Paul, demonstrating rare conviction, drawn from a bruising encounter with the pesticides lobby after an ill-advised short position, loathes them. For the sake of his intellectual pride, he has worked out a business argument to underpin his logic.

"You tell me I have no understanding of nature," he tells Jean, trying not to lose his temper for Bénédicte's sake. "But there is nothing more unnatural than pesticides. Every pest has a natural predator. It's you who is destroying the balance and you're also destroying your business model, such as it is. The next generation already prefers drugs to alcohol; alcohol laced with chemical toxins doesn't stand a chance."

There is no possibility that either will admit to being wrong. Jean simply says: "*Je ne suis pas d'accord,*" and walks away. The son-in-law will never be a son.

4

After a day of limited exercise, Dominique is lying awake in what was once her father's room, staring up as he often has in disbelief that no-one has found the time, energy or inclination to remove the woodchip paper from the beamed, sloping ceiling. It never occurred to him to tackle it himself. Instead it has been painted over and over again in varying shades of white, off-white and cream, all of which fail to mask the ugliness that jars with the blackened beams. At the same time, Dominique is sharing her mother's sense that everything is too small. In the house of *bonne-maman*, as she has always called Claudine, finding people is harder than avoiding them. Meals have gone cold while everyone runs around hunting for *bon-papa*. Dominique, her namesake, was forced to declare herself in games of hide and seek, as Bénédicte and *bonne-maman* have reminisced. The challenge then was to convince Dominique she had won because she had hidden so well when she was convinced no-one had really wanted to find her. Dominique is the shadow that looms over Dominique's life. She's at once hungry to know everything about this rebellious aunt and sick of the knowledge that her own role is to be a substitute when everyone knows that is impossible, especially when she is barred from doing the one thing Dominique loved so much and which she craves. She accepts Bénédicte has also given up horse-riding and that she loved it too, but then, in the opinion of her daughter, Bénédicte, at not yet forty, is old and unfit and was probably just looking for an excuse. Dominique believes that, like the other Dominique, she is a natural horsewoman. Walled up as she is in the insular conservatism of rural Surrey, she also thinks the other Dominique would have shared her fascination with the edgier, urban vein of Englishness; with London and its sharp, ugly fashions and a refusal to conform; the London of Amy Winehouse and David Bowie. She wishes those mythical humans were around to help her interpret these times, but they are even more out of reach than the London they helped to define.

In their absence, Dominique does what typical, modern human beings do when they are feeling lost and takes out her phone. She has no new messages. She turns to social media and finds little comfort in the outpourings as chaotic as life itself. She browses through her list of contacts, finds no-one she could call at this hour and tosses down the phone in disgust. Looking around the modest room, she's drawn to a wooden desk, where she imagines her father somewhat lazily despatched his holiday prep. It's a reduced size roll-top desk that must have always been too small for any serious work, she thinks, but it has compartments that could store all sorts of secrets. For the most part, they contain the usual debris of formative years – fossils, half-used erasers, a rusting pencil sharpener. A larger drawer in the side of the desk is more interesting. There is a school report that confirms the laziness. Paul's art teacher declares "Gray does not try at all". For maths, he has "considerable ability," but fails to show his workings. English literature: wilful refusal to read the texts. He was good at science though. The chemistry teacher was especially impressed by the success of his experiments.

Dominique continues her search. There are exercise books full of her father's messy scrawl. There's a letter opener with a parrot's head brought back from someone's foreign holiday and then there is a bundle of three black, hard-back notebooks tied together with a red ribbon. The ribbon is already intriguing. Paul Gray has very little to do with ribbons. The smell also draws her. It's a smell that is at least a generation older than Paul's schoolbooks. As she undoes the ribbon, Dominique has the sense she has found something to add drama to lockdown as if the sudden ending of everything she has known so far is not dramatic enough. She opens the top one. The name Ida is written inside the cover. She is looking at a diary.

September 1, 1940

They're here now: the children I never had. Mother doesn't approve. She says I'm being selfish and by that, she means I will have less time for her. She might be right that my motives are bad. She would know all about that. Yet I cling to the hope I can still do good. I couldn't have left them there, dressed in their rags in that terrible place. Their father would never have forgiven me. Maybe I did it for him, my clever, handsome cousin driven to an early grave by his crazy wife. Maybe I did it out of guilt because I was the one who got her taken away.

I cannot bear to think of the scene. I write to excise the memory or is it to atone? It was my fault. I raised the alarm. I was sure she would kill them, really, I was. The neighbours had found her by the dank, filthy canal dragging her screaming children behind her. They said she had supernatural strength. They said she was about to throw them in and probably herself too. I was more than ready to believe them.

It's true, I never wanted her to marry my cousin, but I could barely stand the violence of seeing her wrenched from her children, the children she had tried to kill and couldn't endure to be parted from. Jack was banging away on the piano, the only thing in the hovel that was more than a necessity, and Molly sobbed convulsively as they strapped her mother to a stretcher. Florence had just been shopping for probably the last time in her life and the pathetic groceries that she could ill afford spilt on to the floor as if in scorn of her failed attempt to prove to the world she could be a capable, functioning human being.

I can't deny they were a handsome couple, outwardly at least, and the children are good-looking too. Molly has her mother's jet black curls and hazel-green eyes. Jack's blond and blue-eyed, like their father and like me. I think Molly's the brighter. That matters to me enormously, though what good did top of the class do for me? She's by some miracle at grammar school. They told cousin James she had passed the entrance exam as he lay in hospital with hours left to live. He died, they said, of a stomach ulcer, but they may as well have said he died of everything life had thrown at him. Molly was there beside him stunned and then stunned again, barely a year later, when they carried her mother away, screaming, to be locked away perhaps for the rest of her days and all around, there's a war going on, wrecking hundreds of thousands of other lives. When you look at it that way, my gesture is as pointless as it's selfish, but isn't that just nature, human or otherwise – part of a grand scheme or a total waste of time? Even suffering must surely be better than nothingness. It leaves open the possibility of meaning.

Dominique shudders. It's as if a voice has spoken to her from beyond the grave. It has immediacy. It also puzzles her and vexes her. Dominique prides herself on being bilingual, but French is her mother tongue and she cannot quite work out what is happening. She Googles the word dank. She reads the entry again. This writer has taken charge of children whose mother was taken away and whose father has died. They are living through the war occasionally mentioned by her grandparents who had heard of its horrors from their parents. Her father also talks of it, or rather rants about it. He blames Britain's decision to cut itself away from Europe for what he refers to as "ridiculous, mistaken, fake nostalgia" for the "so-called Blitz spirit" and "misguided gratitude to America" for supposedly rescuing us when everyone else had made so many terrible sacrifices. He has also warned her the Surrey neighbours don't necessarily agree with his pro-European sentiments, which begs the question, as Bénédicte has repeatedly observed, of why he has got them all stranded in the middle of them.

Dominique takes up the second book uncertain she can process much more of the first one for now. This one belonged to Molly, one of the two almost-orphaned children.

I was desperate to escape and now I'm here in this tall, dark, winding house with dusty dark corners I dread and too many women and not enough men, just my little brother and he's even more lost than I am. I sat on the stairs long after I was supposedly asleep and heard their conversation, more like remarks just thrown out into the air, startled if they get an answer. Aunt Ida, as we're to call her, though she's really father's cousin, our second cousin, said I was numb. I'm not numb. I'm in pain. As soon as I wake, the first thing I remember is that I have no father and my mother has gone mad. Aunt Ida still has a mother who seems to be driving her mad. I think that's why she wanted us here to share her pain. I'm sure father would have said we should be grateful.

She is at least a blood relation with a reason to care for us even if we're not exactly her own. It's better than that terrible home they threw us in like stray dogs in a pound. It was so noisy, so hectic, so impossible to be alone with your thoughts.

She picks up the third book that belonged to Jack, Molly's little brother. He instantly commands Dominique's sympathy as a human being denied freedom.

She gave us both a notebook and told us to write down our thoughts. She said it would help, but it feels like homework. We're all sitting quietly alone in our own rooms staring at sheets of paper. Molly says lots of people are keeping diaries because this is an important time in history and people in future will want to know how we felt when we're long dead. But I just want to live. No one's going to care what happens to me. I want to run around. I want to be in the fresh air. I don't want to write down things for other people to judge and scoff at.

Dominique carries on reading until at last she falls asleep.

5

Freed from commutes, schooldays and alarm clocks, people in lockdown can wake up whenever they like, as far as Dominique is concerned. Her mother, who, like all old people, always wakes up early anyway, takes a different stance: missing breakfast when you are a guest is rude and you'll achieve nothing in life if you surrender all discipline. Dominique is in for a furious volley of *sotto voce* French when she finally emerges blinking into the early April sunlight. Her brain is still erring on the side of the subconscious, the bottled-up and what she thinks she believes, not what she knows she ought to say. Her retorts inflict maximum damage. "You make it so obvious you scorn grand-mere and that is so much worse than accidentally over-sleeping. Besides, where has your discipline got you?"

Dominique has touched a raw nerve. Bénédicte's almost daily anguish is that she hasn't achieved any more than the female generation before her who could, she imagines, still convince itself that marriage and motherhood was its destiny. She hasn't even married the man of her dreams and she's failed to provide Dominique with the sibling that might rein in her ego. She gives her daughter a basilisk stare.

The stare is universal, but the conversation is all in French, which arguably is also a breach of hospitality. Rowena can't be sure of the literal meaning, but she recognises the force of early teenage rebellion. Partly because she sees her own advantage in getting her grand-daughter on-side, partly because of a practical need to contain the potential anarchy, she swiftly distributes elevenses, a new word to Dominique and one she finds she enjoys. It means rather English-tasting coffee and another of Rowena's cakes, politely declined by Bénédicte, prompting a French aside from Dominique that it is rude to refuse.

Paul, meanwhile, has found this is a convenient moment to disappear and he is heading for Bart's favourite bench, which is just about a permitted lockdown exercise walk away. Bart is there waiting with a flask of coffee, having decided that cans of lager in the morning were too sleazy even for two burnt-out City traders. He threw in a slug of cognac, though, in the spirit of *caffe corretto* and on the premise that if alcohol in hand sanitisers kills the virus, then brandy in one's coffee is worth a shot.

Paul sits down cautiously as far away from Bart as the bench will allow and accepts the offer of coffee, wondering if that's high risk. Bart reads his mind.

"Don't worry mate. I have a separate cup. Can't be too careful, though all this is seriously uncool."

"Thanks," says Paul. He is on edge, literally as well as metaphorically. Bart and he lead each other astray, especially when they're bored.

"How's Bénédicte getting on with your mother?" asks Bart, the tiniest hint of insinuation in his voice.

"I was more worried about Bénédicte and Dominique when I left. You know how it is... teenagers.... and Bénédicte was a bit hard on her. I suppose everyone's uptight and rebellion becomes more complicated when you have to decide which language to rebel in."

"Yeah," says Bart, sipping his coffee and now wishing it were beer. "We have the same problem and it's seriously unhealthy being cooped up like this. You need to get out and meet people."

"So, how's your happy household?" asked Paul, taking his cue.

"Good days and bad days," says Bart. "Tiny things feel like major setbacks and small things cheer us up. It's a rollercoaster. If the internet crashes, it's a full-scale catastrophe. On the other hand, coming back from the supermarket with the stuff you actually wanted can improve the collective mood more than you would ever have believed in our previous lives when the cupboard was fully stocked."

"Nothing like learning not to take anything for granted, as my mother would say, though we can't help ourselves" Paul says wryly. "Do you know anyone who's actually had it?"

"They're not sure. Testing's so chaotic. I don't know anyone who's died of it. It's hard to know what to believe."

Paul lets that remark go. He's not going to get into the camp of conspiracy and pandemic denial that he suspects might appeal to Bart as an excuse to cast caution to the winds and buy Bitcoin. If the internet is a guide, there are people who really believe every government has shut down its economy because of an international conspiracy and that the daily death toll is a list of political assassinations in disguise. Personally, he's convinced at some point a pandemic was inevitable, but he still feels the absurdity of meeting Bart covertly on a bench with a flask of laced coffee as if they're two old men.

It's also inevitable that Bart will turn the conversation to trade and it happens sooner rather than later.

"I was thinking there is a trade in all this," is Bart's next remark.

"There's a surprise," says Paul. He doesn't admit he has been thinking the same.

"Shorting travel shares. Maybe a bit obvious, but isn't this just the perfect excuse for companies to axe all that business-class gadding about and at this rate, ordinary people won't have the money to go anywhere even when they can? The only way for the travel market to go is down."

"It's not just travel shares that will tank," says Paul. "It's all the not strictly necessary stuff this stupid country is built on. The high street's had it. No-one needs new clothes. All those City sandwich shops are toast."

"Very funny," says Bart. "But, you're right, there's the potential for quite a portfolio."

"Illegal cognac had more of a thrill," says Paul.

"Yes, but that trade nearly got us killed."

"Somehow, I think it still could," says Paul.

"What do you mean? It was years ago."

"There are people who would still do me in given half a chance."

"Nah," says Bart. "They've moved on. With any luck, they've caught the plague."

Momentarily, they sip their coffee in silence. In the days when social silences were rare, the French would have said an angel was passing.

"Don't you think we've made enough money?" asks Paul at last.

"It's all very well for you to say. You married an heiress. I married a woman who will never feel financially secure until we have enough to buy our way out of any situation. Actually, scrub that. She will NEVER feel financially secure. She needs to know we can afford school fees and medical bills. At this rate, we might even need our own island and a private jet. You can't fob her off with the old money-can't-buy-happiness line."

"If no amount is enough, getting in over your head is a bit pointless," Paul mutters.

"Oh, come on, mate. Have you actually got anything better to do?" pleads Bart.

"This could be our great chance to mend our ways. Adapt or die when the whole world is having to," Paul almost pleads.

"You know we're both more likely to die than adapt. This is what we do. It's too late to re-programme."

"I suppose I could make a few calls," says Paul. "But right now, I'd better get back and face the music."

6

The music is discordant. Bénédicte is furious with Paul for leaving her alone to contend with two enemy forces. If she were an angry young man, she would probably have run away and punched the first person she met. As it is, she has left Rowena and Dominique to bond over spring planting decisions and she is hiding away with her iPad in pursuit of solace and solutions. That she knows no-one in Surrey is almost academic, given that the only people she is allowed to see are Paul's mother and her immediate family – another interesting English phrase that to her evokes the pressing needs of those around her and that the urgency is temporary. It would still somehow help to know friends were within reach. There is Bart, but Bart could never be trusted not to take Paul's side unless of course they had an affair. She can't deny she'd suspected him of being attracted to her. She asks herself what she would have done had he attracted her. Probably nothing, given how emotionally exhausting she finds her existing relationships, except that, right now, they are not enough to satisfy. She can't stop thinking of François, the one who got away. Intellectually, she knows that happiness is based on cultivating what you have and being grateful; accepting Rowena's strength of character and putting aside their bad start; realising her son in many people's eyes, not just Rowena's, is quite a catch. Paradise, nirvana, emotional maturity, whatever you want to call it, is a state of wise acceptance of limitation and compromise that in any case probably is as good as it gets; the antithesis of that restless desire to escape the imperfection that will accompany you wherever you go. Depending on where you stand, you could say it is extremely dull and unambitious or the highest attainment. From the viewpoint of the typical 21st-century human, she sees the appeal of experimenting with the new and getting a temporary high from fresh appreciation; when the novelty wears off, just move on – the one thing no-one can do right now. Her mind sifts through all the English people she has ever met and she wonders about Polly, the world's least aggressive journalist whom she met all those years ago after she and Paul found themselves facing the glare of the media. They had just stumbled across the body of the man who had been the world's most influential oil minister. But for that extreme incident on the edge of her parents' vineyards, she would never have met Paul or Rowena and she wouldn't have a daughter named after her late sister. Possibly her sister would still be alive and, if she were, Bénédicte would never have been so emotionally vulnerable that marrying Paul would have seemed a good idea.

She can never decide whether the facts of their meeting have kept them together or are grounds for rejecting a relationship that began on the strangest of premises, even assuming there is any right answer. In the continued fall-out of that singular event and all that ensued, Polly had also met that French journalist Pierre. Bénédicte is mildly curious to know whether their *amour* has survived. For some reason, she suspects not, but would any sane person have put money on Paul and she being together more than a decade on? It's all random and viewed through the current lens, suffocatingly local. Based on impulsive decisions, you surround yourself with relationships at which you must work; you are so steeped in blood, as Macbeth would have it, that returning is not an option. As you endure the relationships that surround you, you value people you never see far more, but the unseen will wither and die of neglect. Contact that isn't face to face or physical is never enough unless there is the sinister hopefulness, however subliminal, of some mercenary motive. Maybe that's it, Polly was just after a story. From her lockdown prison, Bénédicte is willing to run the risk that even Polly had ulterior motives. She digs out Polly's email and writes the briefest of messages, partly because her writing is self-conscious in English and partly to conserve her efforts as she is about 50% sure she will get an "address no longer valid" bounce-back.

Dear Polly,

I hope you are well? I know that's a big question at the moment.

I've often wondered how you were and now I'm wondering from Surrey, where Paul has got us locked down/up/in (you know I can never master English prepositions) with his delightful mother.

I know we can't meet but let me know your news. Maybe we could chat some time?

Bénédicte x

The kiss is an afterthought. The French throw them around physically, although that could be a thing of the past, while the Anglo Saxons are generous with them in their correspondence when there is no risk of spreading germs. Bénédicte decides that one little letter could only be damaging were she writing to her boss or to Bart. It does not bounce back.

7

Rowena's calculation was astute. Having fallen out with her mother, Dominique is at her disposal to help with planting beetroot, chard and radish seeds. Both wonder whether they will still be confined to Surrey by the time their seeds are plants. Dominique feels suspended in time and place between the *potager* of *bonne-maman*, where she has often been sent to collect an ingredient or asked to help with the weeding, and the vegetable plot of *grand-mère*. It sits next to a reproduction Edwardian greenhouse that is the envy of her neighbours and, as in Cognac, it is on chalk soil. Dominique hasn't previously articulated that her parents' families are united by limestone, but she has grown up with the idea of *terroir*. *Bon-papa* has even explained to her in the moments of lyricism that occasionally break through his mournful taciturnity that *terroir* means an attachment to the *terre*; that you are defined by where you come from. It's a form of fatalism. He is talking merely about place, but Dominique reckons time is at least as important. She's thinking about the diaries and whether to broach the subject with *grand-mère*, who, now she thinks about it, could have had jetblack curls in her youth and still has hazel-green eyes. She decides she'd rather read to the end first.

Bonne-maman is sowing seeds into dry, grey soil in her *potager* which, logically, should be near the kitchen, but instead is tucked away in a scrap of land reached through a gateway in one of the many limestone walls that surround and divide their property in the Grand Champagne growing area. It has its own, hard-to-define atmosphere. In a city, it would be *terrain vague*, a residual, marginal, transitional, overlooked area that defies classification. Its purpose is to have no obvious purpose. So-called civilisation has been and gone or has yet to arrive. In her *terrain vague*, Claudine feels cut off from the world and that pleases her rather than not. The world can come to her if it wants. She has achieved the calm stasis Bénédicte associates with human happiness, except Claudine's calm is dangerously close to emotional deadness and her core relationship is based on a parallel not a shared life. Those she loves, she loves out of habit. Loss has taught her to limit how much she cares.

Her mind processes a muddle of half-thoughts. She still has the images of *Le Cercle Rouge* in her mind. As the only newish thing to enter her consciousness in weeks, she is worrying away at their meaning or lack of meaning.

Whatever significance its director intended never penetrated through the personal meaning for Claudine as she broached the threshold of marriage with a man whom, even then, she did not associate with thrill and adventure. The steady, occasionally flinty Jean is grey, like the soil beneath her fingers that in turn makes her think of the bleak, anonymous fields in the middle of nowhere where some of Melville's filming took place, except those fields were wet. The soil here is bone dry and almost the colour of bone. As she waters in her seeds, it temporarily turns from light to dark grey.

Jean is of course tending his vines. They look healthy, but he knows the dangers. Every Cognac *viticulteur* is haunted still by the collective trauma of phylloxera, the pest that once wiped out the vineyard. Recovery took years and relied on new root stock from America. The old vineyard is extinct. If there had been a chemical to destroy the phylloxera louse everyone would have used it as a matter of survival. Jean thinks of his uneasy conversation with his son-in-law whom he didn't have down as an eco-warrior. That had supposedly been the role of Thomas Fischer, his other daughter's man until he turned out to be an internationally wanted criminal. He doesn't rule out that Bénédicte's choice is just as bad.

8

For the first time in weeks, Paul is on a bike. It's not his favourite bike. That is in a barn in Cognac. There are moments when he feels almost vertiginously insecure about the parts of the life he has abandoned in France. It is they, not he, that are falling – further and further from his grasp, like dreams fading in daylight or once-vivid memories, receding into the pit of oblivion until it's as if they never were. He cannot feel secure in the present moment because it's impossible to unite everything he has liked about his life so far in the here and now. Instead, it seems, everything he hasn't liked, hated even, is crowding in. He is furious with himself for failing to pack his carbon-framed bike when he embarked on his scramble to Surrey. The long-discarded teenage bike that he has taken apart and put back together again in the slower time of lockdown is reminding him of his age and the still-twinging hip that will never quite recover from his fall down the twenty-four steps of Darking station that he blames on Fischer – caught on CCTV at the scene, or so his mother has told everyone she knows. The police were not very interested then and they are certainly not now as they battle to contain the mounting anger of a bitterly divided population stuck in bitterly divided households. Paul thinks the Grays aren't faring so badly. His mother and Bénédicte will never get on, but then he will never agree with her father about how vines should be cultivated and he has managed to convince himself that Bénédicte has accepted that. He's more worried about Bart, he thinks, and he has enough self-knowledge to be aware he is using Bart's unhappiness as an excuse to justify another foolish venture. From habit, he can't help working out a few trading positions as he cycles up and down one of the many hills of Darking. They mean that whichever direction you take, you quickly meet an unpleasantly challenging incline or a dead-end. Only a long, arduous haul will allow a sense of escape.

After his final descent of the day, Paul decides on a modest detour via Bart's bench – just in case. Bart probably won't be there, but he could enjoy the view. He's slowing to get off and park his bike when he sees someone who is not Bart has beaten him to the spot. Typical, he thinks. Even in lockdown, a bench with a view on a pleasant early evening is occupied. Apparently, it is a tramp and he has plonked a filthy great bag beside him to mark his territory, but Paul feels a troubling sense of recognition. He is hoping it's paranoia when the owner of the head with a tangle of long, unwashed hair turns towards him and meets his eyes. He sees an older, more haggard Thomas Fischer. In a surge of adrenaline, he cycles off. He no longer notices his twinging hip.

9

*T*oday was exciting, reads Dominique.

Aunt Ida took us to work with her. She said she couldn't leave us with her mother and we have no school until Monday. I'd rather go to work. She runs a jewellery factory with her brother, full of gold and diamonds. We went there by tram to the part of town where there are lots of jewellery makers. They don't make as much jewellery these days because of the war, but still Aunt Ida said the trade goes on and people who have money want to put it into beautiful, precious things that they can carry and hide. She said it gave them hope. It made them feel less helpless. And then she told us how diamonds are symbols of eternity because they were created millions of years ago deep inside the earth and they last forever.

That is Jack, so far, Dominique's favourite of the new characters in her pared-back life. She turns to the same day in Molly's diary – September 5, 1940, just before The Blitz her father has ranted about from time to time. If Jack is the reluctant pupil, like Dominique, who should right now be doing her online schoolwork, Molly is the conscientious student.

Jack was happy today. He loved the jewellery factory. I thought he'd think it was too girly, but it's true it was an adventure. There were many things that weren't girly at all. Most of the staff were men, soldering and beating out shapes, while the women added in the stones and sometimes made tea. They were a proper community who understood each other without saying very much, so different from being forced together in this house, silent and grudging and full of wilful misunderstanding.

In a way we shouldn't have gone, though that's what made it so exciting. Everyone knows the jewellery quarter is a target because some of the factories are making ammunition, but Aunt Ida said their factory is too small for anyone to notice and we could always hide under the stairs. She's different at work. She defers to her brother but everyone else looks up to her. They call her Miss Ida and he's Mr Leonard just in case anyone might think they were husband and wife. He keeps order among the staff, making sure they don't take any diamonds home in their trouser pockets or even in their turn-ups, and Aunt Ida does the books. She's really good at maths and Uncle Leonard said she's also good at buying stones. He said she has a sharp eye and has bought diamonds they sold to important customers. He said that was why they've been allowed to carry on working even in the war and of course Uncle Leonard's too old to fight, but he has a son who's a pilot and I know he's worried sick about him and I've heard Aunt Ida praying for him. It's strange to be making beautiful sparkly things only streets away from the factory that might make the bombs his son drops and it's sad that Aunt Ida spends so much time buying diamonds when no-one has ever bought her one.

The atmosphere was almost merry on the tram home with the three of us. Aunt Ida was as excited as Jack. She told him how diamonds were created millions of years ago and she sparkled herself, but then we entered this tall, dark house dominated by her mother. To us all, she's just Aunt Ida's stern mother who has been widowed since the first World War that left Aunt Ida fatherless. She exuded spiteful disapproval. She'd been alone and we'd been together.

Dominique finds herself overwhelmed by sadness. She can't work out how much is for herself and how much is for these people so dead and impossible to interrogate they might as well be fictional. Maybe, her sorrow is even for humankind's collective failure, built from millions of individual failures, as everyone flails around, living together and living apart, never really able to share sorrow or even happiness, lost in private worlds and occasionally enjoying moments of solidarity – in a diamond factory in the middle of a war. It's as if they all desperately needed a sparkle of supposedly unnecessary luxury.

She reads on. Jack is partly right. She doesn't always find his thoughts fascinating, but she wants to read about the nights in the makeshift air-raid shelter as Ida's mother snored while the bombs rained down. Her own reality is different only in style. The fundamental content of tensions between incompatible people is the same.

10

Bénédicte is reading too. She has an email from Polly, who says she's thrilled to hear from her. Is that because she's English and polite or because any glimmer of friendliness in times of pestilence at least raises the prospect of healthy human contact? Polly is in London. Paris and Pierre are not mentioned. She's still editing and says she minds less *now no-one can really run around enjoying the action*, as she puts it. That tells Bénédicte that for all her played-down ambition, Polly's happiness has always depended as much as the next person's on feeling she had succeeded relative to everyone else: if no-one is notching up major scoops, Polly is content, it would seem. She asks Bénédicte if she's still in touch with Reem, the third and highest achieving member of that circle of friendship that briefly formed in the ripple of events that surrounded Bénédicte's meeting Paul and that was half-heartedly maintained until the energy that created it dispersed. Now perhaps it could re-form.

Bénédicte laboriously crafts her reply, slowed by her anxious, non-native questioning of whether she has struck the right tone. Polly's French is at least as good as Bénédicte's English but English has become their language of communication, just as with Paul, except in decreasingly rare moments of tenderness when he endeavours to charm her with his still imperfect French – or when they need to exclude his mother, who, Bénédicte fears, understands far more than she lets on.

Dear Polly,

You've made my day. Selfishly, I'm very happy you're in London because surely at some point soon we can meet? Or maybe we could be modern, find Reem and organise a call?

Bénédicte x

A call would be a desperate second best. Conference calls are for work, for transactional exchanges of information. Friendship, she thinks, thrives when any motives are disguised by fun, pleasure and excitement, just as when the three of them met a decade ago in Brown's Hotel. Even then, she knew Reem, the outstanding Saudi scientist, was calculating how to avenge the death of her beloved Saudi oil minister and somehow thought Polly and she could help, but that was a minor consideration compared with the desire to luxuriate in the atmosphere of old, well-healed London, sip Orange Pekoe tea and nibble on ridiculously small sandwiches. Were she an absolute puritan, Bénédicte would conclude relationships that rely on concealment are worthless. Instead, she leans to the view absolute truth is impossible because how can you even know what it is.

That is fortunate for Paul who choses that moment to walk in.

"You look as if you've seen a ghost," observes Bénédicte.

"I'm hoping it was just a figment of my guilty conscience," says Paul. "But I fear I've just seen someone I hoped I'd never see again."

Bénédicte is always charmed, flattered even, when he entrusts her with his vulnerability. In their new Surrey context, she is also relieved he has sought out her, not his mother, though he may do that too.

11

"It will be yours one day," Rowena solemnly tells Dominique, who has chosen to admire her grandmother's solitaire engagement ring as she has taken it off and put it into a pot she keeps for the purpose on the window ledge of her perfectly ordered kitchen. She is making pastry and is anxious to prevent the diamond ring she almost always wears losing its lustre from a coating of flour.

"It needs to stay in the family," Rowena says. "It has a long history." Once allergic to the lyrical nostalgia in which *grand-mère* tends to indulge, Dominique's lockdown reading has left her ready to be drawn in.

"It was my mother's engagement ring. She never married."

For Mrs Rowena Gray, this is a revelation, delivered with abrupt drama. It is also something of a plot spoiler as Dominique has yet to discover that from the diaries. She says nothing as she sits on a chair next to the pastry table ignoring the incoming messages she can hear buzzing into her phone. She's sure *grand-mère* will continue with her story now she has started. Dominique is used to kitchens being the place where women narrate to other women. It happens in Cognac and she assumes it happens in Surrey. The calmness of Rowena's task of rubbing butter into flour, performed thousands of times in a lifetime, releases her from her usual social performance. The accumulated bitterness and misguided conviction are still there, but without their customary menace. The guard, always up in Bénédicte's presence, is down. She is doing little more than thinking aloud with no concern for whether her burst of sentences makes sense to anyone else. It's almost as if she has rehearsed the version of the events that she considers formed her in previous, solitary pastry sessions or as she weeded her flower border.

"I wasn't a mistake though. I was desperately wanted. Some people say my name means joy in old English. It was my father's mother's name, my link to him. I was teased mercilessly for it at school by all the Janes and Marys and Elizabeths. It was character-forming. I thought they might at least have given it to you as a middle name, but Paul tells me the French have problems with ws or should I say double vs?"

"*Double v*," Dominique says quietly.

"Whether double v or double u, for me it stands for war.

They would have married had he survived the war. No-one would have blamed them for not waiting, but of course I had to spend my childhood pretending they had been married, just as she had spent her childhood pretending her mother was dead."

"Why did she do that?" asks Dominique, though she suspects she knows.

"Her mother was locked away. She was a dangerous schizophrenic. The shame was overwhelming. My mother never could talk about it."

"That's not healthy," observes Dominique. She's thinking of her dead aunt. She is mentioned, but her invisible presence prevents them from being the kind of normal happy family Dominique believes exists somewhere. Almost everything is done with the other Dominique in mind.

"It was what people did then. They shut up and carried on. There was little choice. Nearly everyone had suffered. Wallowing in all this therapy is just an indulgence."

This would be the moment when Bénédicte would bridle and either stifle or fail to stifle the urge to point out that collective trauma had created a bitter, pent-up generation that begrudges happiness and the danger of these times is that it's happening all over again. Depending on how ruthless her mood, Rowena might then question whether years of counselling has reconciled Bénédicte to the loss of her sister and Bénédicte would probably just leave the room with an audible sigh. Paul has been the helpless spectator of many such moments. His mother will never admit blame and Bénédicte will not forgive.

Dominique says nothing in her youthful indifference and Rowena carries on. She has put the pastry mix to chill and she's working on the filling for a chicken and mushroom pie – another English classic that Paul will love and Bénédicte will loathe, while Dominique will toy with the idea of vegetarianism and decide it will have to wait for more auspicious times.

"My mother for one would have said therapy was no use. She knew what was wrong. She'd been cheated of a mother and a father, but especially a mother. The minute she found someone to love, war snatched him away. All she could do was be for me the mother she never had, but that meant giving up all the hopes her teachers had nurtured of a university degree and she resented that. She also had to carry on living with Ida and her mother when she was desperate to carve out her own life, but how could she when she had to look after me?"

She pauses to reach for the pepper grinder and declares: "Extra pepper for your mother." Dominique can't tell whether she is being kindly or grudging, so she lets the remark pass.

"Tell me about the ring," she says.

"It's a beautiful South African stone. Ida fetched it from South Africa in the middle of the war. It was an epic journey in so many ways."

Dominique has read about this and realises the moment to admit she has found the diaries has passed. The journey fascinated her all the more because she has less freedom to travel than during a period that until now had represented the most deprived of times. Ida had left behind Molly and Jack with her mother in that dark house, while she went off to buy diamonds from a family she knew from when they had lived in Antwerp. They were her best contact in the industry and they'd fled occupied Belgium for South Africa to hide away on a remote farm, hoping no-one would notice that they were Jewish. While Ida was airsick in a military plane or marvelling at the big skies of the veld, Molly had snatched meetings with Andrew, Ida's nephew, the pilot. She was only fourteen then, the age of Shakespeare's Juliet, as Dominique has learnt from a school trip to the theatre that she now knows she didn't appreciate enough at the time. Molly was nineteen when Rowena emerged screaming into the world, just after the war had ended and weeks after Andrew had been killed. Dominique struggles with the idea that the solid Rowena was born of tragic romance. Then again, she supposes, all love, all life ultimately ends in tragedy if you believe the individual matters. Maybe love is best avoided altogether. There doesn't seem much point in a future generation from where she sits, so why bother with extreme emotional pain? And while you're at it, why not do away with plans and reminiscence and live, goldfish-like, entirely in the present? Is it because even the present seems as much about place as time?

12

The texts that have buzzed into Dominique's phone are from her schoolfriends. They want to compare notes on homework. They want to know about lockdown in Surrey, as opposed to lockdown in Cognac. They want to be distracted. They want to know what life is like somewhere else. Dominique in some moods would seize on them eagerly. For now, she ignores them as faint echoes from a retreating life. They seem further than a few hundred miles away and no more real than Molly and Andrew. She slips out of the kitchen for more reading and a retreat from the other Dominique into another dysfunctional family. She starts with Ida on a Sunday. They've been to church. Ida is agonising over her sense of disbelief. She knows that people are dying in horrible circumstances, but she can only apprehend her own here and now. It's part of the survival instinct.

Leonard came for lunch and brought with him a breath of fresh air and his son Andrew, who's on leave. We went for a walk along the canal. It's dangerous territory. It reminds me of how this all began and I wonder if the children think it too, but I don't dare to ask them.

There is a pair of swans there I've watched for months. In defiance of everything, they float along together, unsullied by the filthy canal, and mutually devoted. To each other, they are irreplaceable, whereas I cannot tell one from the other. They are wonderful, but they are swans like any others, almost unnatural with their rubbery feet and stiff, sculpted bearing, until every now and then, they bend their heads to puzzle slightly stupidly over some unexpected obstacle or to wiggle their pure white tails coquettishly.

There's an eerie duality that allows the swans and their peace to coexist with war and soldiers who kill indiscriminately, while lovers and parents love uncritically. If they saw their targets as individuals, no-one could kill. If they see a dispensable mass, they can hate. Florence's madness is a collapse of whatever fragile structure supports that duality. It's as if the cells of hate have taken over the ones of devotion in a coup of the mind or perhaps she has just lost her faith that there is even any difference and ultimately, hate, love and madness are all ways of refusing to see clearly when reality is unbearable.

The swans echo my childlessness. I saw them build a nest, lay an egg and then abandon it unhatched. It lay there for weeks like any old lifeless piece of rubbish. They moved to another site, tried again and failed again while all the coots and moorhens effortlessly produced balls of sooty, squeaking fluff that have since grown and fledged. Still the swans sail on superior and serene, apparently unchanged by war or personal failure, keen enough if you throw them a few crumbs but indifferent and self-contained if you don't. Would that I could be so stoical. Maybe I could be if I couldn't speak.

While Ida is lost in her thoughts, Molly is falling in love with yet another precious only child. Her diary entry doesn't mention the church or the canal or the swans or anything but feelings.

It can't be possible to be in love when you've only met someone once and especially when it's your cousin or nearly your cousin. What is he to me exactly? If Uncle Leonard's my father's cousin's brother, that makes him my father's cousin too, so Andrew's my second cousin once removed or something. That's not that close, but still blood. Besides, I'm only fourteen, just a silly girl, and he's twenty-two and a hero and must have scores of women throwing themselves at his feet. And it's probably just because I've been cooped up in this suffocating house with ageing women and my little brother that I'm so desperate for something good. But my heart is racing and I've never felt like this before. I close my eyes and I see his somehow familiar face and his dashing uniform. I think I must have met him before, though our parents were so strange we didn't see many relatives, not even Aunt Ida until she took over our lives. If I have met him, we were both so much younger, almost different people in a different life, and I was too young to feel this wild confusion. I don't know whether I can stand the embarrassment of ever seeing him again when my blushes give me away. Maybe I won't see him again and I couldn't bear that either. It's unthinkable that he could be shot down and yet I know it's a miracle he hasn't been yet. Uncle Leonard was subdued as if he couldn't enjoy being with his son, his only son, for fear of losing him. He's the one precious heir.

Dominique flicks through. She's ignoring the accounts of Jack's fights at school and his hours of piano practice that interrupt Molly's reading and letter-writing. She races on to her favourite part: Ida's journey to Africa when Molly and Andrew managed to meet again, away from Ida's watchful eyes, and Ida found richness and enjoyment in impossible times. She even drank enough to suffer the one hangover mentioned in the diaries.

It feels all wrong now – and it's not just because of the hangover. Last night was magical and unreal, a throw-back to those pre-war parties that released so much tension until no-one could deny the politics anymore.

While the bombs pounded Britain and the Germans occupied half of Europe and Leonard thought I was being brave and self-sacrificing, we were sitting outside looking at the distant hills and the deep red African sunset and drinking champagne. It was as if we had collectively decided to take a break from worrying and from trying to mend what we cannot fix, or perhaps it's just that human nature is unable to sustain any one state, especially not of despair and stay alive. In any case, we celebrated disproportionately what was a deal big for me but small for people as grand as they are.

They probably have parties like this all the time in a desperate attempt to shut out the horror and perhaps they assume, like their ancestors, the great Europeans of centuries past, that peace will soon be negotiated.

I'm sure they condescended to me and my humble, parochial, middle-class anxiety. They might have secretly been toasting something entirely different and letting me believe it was about my little deal. I didn't care. Briefly, I ceased to worry about the long, exhausting journey home, carrying a valuable cargo, to my self-inflicted duties; of Molly and Andrew, Jack's piano-playing, mother's health.

I had very little sense of where we were. Agnes and Ralph had met me with a car in Durban and we had driven miles beneath endless skies to the estate, where they are riding out the war. With their usual style, they managed to escape Antwerp just before the occupation. They had connections because of the diamond business and I suppose through the close-knit Jewish network no-one dares to mention. They even managed to bring over some of their Flemish art that is hanging on the walls of what they modestly call their farmhouse. I felt I was inhabiting one of those paintings, full of symbolism, hidden meaning and aristocrats winking their superior understanding and never sharing it.

Dominque is trying to imagine those paintings when Bénédicte's knock on the door summons her to the present: a dinner of chicken and mushroom pie made by the cook with the diamond ring.

BARBARA LEWIS

13

Polly dines alone in London. It's her staple meal of pasta and pesto, with added cheese, walnuts and an extra dash of olive oil. On Fridays and Saturdays, she allows herself a glass of wine with it, but she always stops at one. She knows the dangers. She doesn't want to be one of those sad, lonely lockdown people consoling themselves with drink. She hadn't even felt the need. She's amazed how little she misses the office, foreign travel, the cycle of professional and personal meetings that seemed endless and important until it abruptly stopped. She's found solace in the strip of garden that belongs to her ground floor flat. She has watched daffodils and tulips bloom and for the first time in her life noticed that tulips open after dawn and close again at nightfall. She marvels that she had not known that before and wonders what else she is still failing to see. Freed from her commute and, with her work confined to busy, eight-hour editing shifts at home, rather than expanding to fill the available time, she has newfound leisure to walk round the local common and relish overheard fragments of conversation. They are more diverse than the office gossip, if disappointingly banal. She lives in the hope of overhearing something salacious. So far, it has been schoolchildren repeating, she imagines, the views of their parents, with amateur swearing thrown in for added swagger. They lament that the prime minister has fucking survived the plague. He deserved to get it. He didn't deserve to survive it. They boast about the heroic front-line workers in their families. She listens to the outdoor exercisers, deprived of their gyms, and meting out advice on the best running routes. People are curiously upbeat, though she supposes the ones out and about are mostly the more positive and pro-active. She would have considered herself one of them, except hearing from Bénédicte has unsettled her. It has thrown her back to a time when she believed she had the potential to become more than she was. Then she still strived for the occasional scoop and for a happy-ever-after relationship. In retrospect, all those months of dashing back and forth to Paris to see Pierre amounted to, in his words, *un acte manqué*. She has struggled to work out what he meant. An embarrassing mistake, she supposes. It isn't flattering, but at least she's released from all the lingering over gourmet meals that made her loathe herself for what she saw as wasted time and energy.

Thoughts of Bénédicte and Pierre lead naturally to Reem. She always felt she had failed Reem. Reem wanted justice for the murdered oil minister who had helped her to become an expert in renewable energy. Polly was never convinced the relationship was healthy. She imagined Reem was a way for the minister to salve his conscience. She possibly served several semi-articulated ends. He was seen to promote a young woman and an alternative to oil. He was providing his country with a future and pacifying his climate critics. The cynical view would be that he patronisingly chose a woman because he did not take green energy seriously, but if he considered Reem a token gesture, he had underestimated her. Pasta barely digested, Polly embarks on an email to Reem, recalling the shyness she always feels, imaging Reem will scornfully probe the limits of her intelligence and the laziness of her assumptions.

Dear Reem,

How are you? Where are you? I hope you're somewhere safe. I'm being very boring and cowardly, editing from home. I know I'm lucky. I have a small garden and I live near a common.

I thought you'd be interested that I've heard from Bénédicte. She emailed me and she's just sent me a text. They're all locked down with Paul's mother in Surrey. She's finding it quite a strain and so, it seems, is Paul. Her text says Paul thinks he has seen Fischer. I thought he was meant to be in jail in Saudi Arabia. Maybe not or maybe Paul is being paranoid, though I've always thought him too arrogant to be a nervous type.

Anyway, it would be lovely to hear from you. Bénédicte thought we could even have a Zoom chat if you felt like it.

Take care,

Polly

Polly closes her laptop to take up a book. She's re-reading Shakespeare from start to finish. Her longing for theatre is almost a physical ache. More than anything theatre could take her away from whatever problems she was wrestling with. However bad her day had been, an evening at the theatre would immerse her in another world. However fictional the characters and plot, a live performance became the all-absorbing present reality. Even a bad production could transport her as she lived and breathed the painful tension of a cast struggling on. Online recordings are not the same, so she settles down with the text, half-tempted to enrol for another degree and get it right this time. She'd have the wisdom of experience, but she wouldn't have the idealism of youth. She would no longer stay up all night developing "almost brilliant" theories, as one of her tutors once described her efforts. To this day, she's not sure whether that also meant they were borderline mad.

Shakespeare blows her mind with his ability to be all-encompassing and yet to understand, in total contrast to the scraps of possible truth that fill her days. He has no solutions though, unless you consider his art was the answer; the very act of articulation was enough to show us the best we can do is to perfect our own lives as he honed his art. We emerge from tragedy with a sense of renewal. Someone noble steps forward to rebuild from the devastation. Maybe it was just a sop. The discord was more compelling. Even so, Polly feels it mattered less then that he couldn't definitively reform human nature when he was worrying about man's damage to man, not to the planet. She wonders if he would have even written had he been born now. He might have been a naturalist, not a humanist.

14

It's the 75th anniversary of Victory in Europe. In normal times, Dominique has regarded May 8 as just one of the bank holidays that, especially in France, make May her favourite month. They inject more energy than the sustained leisure of the summer months. Work, in a typical May, seems to assume its proper place as a contrast to heighten pleasure. But until now, the promise of nature in early bloom, at least on a conscious level, had passed Dominique by. Also, for the first time, she has grasped some of the painful significance of the first VE Day as a desperate, choked-up attempt to revive national morale after years of suffering and when victory was pyrrhic and incomplete. She knows Molly was heart-broken and soon to be the mother of Rowena, whose bitter-sweet arrival meant she was trapped with Ida and her ancient mother. She considers the unprocessed emotional torture that surrounded the birth has made her *grand-mère* sour and difficult, but she does not allow that to affect their bond. According to one of the intricate rules of relationships, if someone somehow acquires the role of lightning conductor – in this case, Bénédicte – those around – namely, Paul and Dominique – can relax and get along with the thunder god or goddess. Dominique thinks, not quite smugly, that being an only child has prepared her for this. Her mother doesn't count. She grew up with a sibling and until now, Dominique had envied her that. Dominique extends the Gray history of isolated egos, brought up among adults rather than surrounded by peers and adept at relying only on themselves to skirt round the older generation's stubborn ways and obsession with asserting control in a desperate defiance of the odds. She perceives *grand-mère* as just an extreme example of the inflexibility, physical and mental, of hardened age.

Grand-mère is in her kitchen listening, teary-eyed, to the radio. On the table she uses to roll out her pastry a local life-style magazine is open at an article suggesting permissible celebrations for VE Day in lockdown. The household is united in considering none has any appeal. They view decking the house in union flags with horror for varying reasons. Rowena regards it as working class and Paul and Bénédicte are appalled by the nationalist overtones. Equally, dressing up in 1940s clothes and waltzing round the garden is hardly going to make this bubble of people feel better about all the things they can't do.

Paul and Bart, who would normally scorn any form of anniversary celebration, birthdays included, have decided they have an excuse to unite their two households. Rowena is staying at home, while Paul, Bénédicte and Dominique are venturing into the garden of the Bartholomew family – hence Bart to his friends, James to his wife – to meet

Agnieszka, Poppy and Daisy. They have solemnly promised Rowena they will all keep their distance and spend every second of their time outside in the fresh, cleansing air. As she doesn't hesitate to remind them, they would never forgive themselves if they infected someone as old and vulnerable as she is.

Dominique considers *grand-mère* indestructible. She is nervous for other reasons. She is aware that part of her finds life more relaxing without the pressure of mingling with contemporaries whom she regards as competitors rather than friends; they compel her into a scramble to know the things they know, but slightly more, and to like only the things they like, as decreed by some mysterious arbiter of taste. Poppy and Daisy are fifteen and twelve, which makes her slightly older than Daisy and younger than Poppy. Getting on with both could be complicated, assuming she can get on with either and that one or the other or both won't see her as a threat encroaching on their territory.

She thinks of the parallel lives of the diaries and has a superstition their patterns will replicate themselves, albeit in a mutated form, like a virus determined to survive, or just because there are only so many kaleidoscopic combinations of behaviour and events, or because a family's past has almost genetic power over a family's future. Apart from her thunderbolt love story, Molly's big relationship so far is with schoolfriend Margaret, one of two sisters, and it is fraught. It has triggered the jealousy that is never far from any relationship as far as Dominique can tell. The sister Joan resents Molly's friendship with Margaret. Margaret and Molly go for walks together, gossip together, puzzle over their homework together. Molly has been invited to tea but there has been no reciprocation as Molly fears to bring anyone into Ida's house. Not without jealousy, Ida has declared they are "thick as thieves" and Joan agrees.

"You like Molly more than you like your own sister," Joan storms in everyone's earshot. Forced to choose, Margaret decides she must put "blood before water," as Molly puts it, another English concept for Dominique. Shattered by the intensity of it all, Molly confides in Ida, who provides an attempted consolation. "All quarrels have stupid petty origins that you couldn't explain to anyone else if they asked about them. Sometimes they even lead to war."

From her vantage point of a dispassionate observer, Dominique finds she has another excuse to conclude that most human relations are best avoided and achieving something bad is much easier than attaining something fragile and good.

With Ida's words preying on her mind, Dominique for the first time in weeks, must also decide what to wear. To the non-discerning eye, her choice is remarkably similar to what she has worn since March, but her French peers would instantly appraise the perfect cut of her jeans, which sit on her narrow hips and have an artful tear just below the right knee. She's also wearing a Stella McCartney ethical cotton T-shirt with strict instructions from her mother not to spill anything on it.

Bénédicte sympathises with her daughter's self-consciousness. She hasn't had a hair cut in months and her favourite clothes are in France. She resorts to securing her hair in a velvet clasp she bought years ago in Paris and has rediscovered in her travel bag of toiletries. She wears the simplest of silk shift dresses that reveals her still enviable figure, while Paul is far too worried about the prospect of proximity to admire the improvised elegance of his wife.

Craving only disguise, he hides behind sunglasses and seriously contemplates donning a mask as the three set off on foot, glad of any form of exercise. It's a glorious day. Dominique thinks of Ida's struggle, not just with Molly and Margaret but with the disjunction between the serene beauty of her swans and the devastation she knew was happening elsewhere. Staring up at clear blue skies, unmarked by contrails, it's an effort to remember that human society is under threat. A form of denial, it's almost the opposite of the willing suspension of disbelief, one of the ideas Dominique's ambitious literature teacher, who believes words are worlds and concepts are cosmoses, has endeavoured to convey.

Paul can barely see the blue skies. He has also completely forgotten about the risk of catching a highly contagious virus and passing it on to his mother, so obsessed is he by the idea that Fischer, his own personal plague, is around every corner. The normally taciturn Bénédicte, somewhat aware of his qualms, is talking nervously. It reminds him with a pang of the excitement of their early acquaintance.

"It will be interesting to meet Bart's wife," she says. "And to have a conversation with someone who doesn't have Gray genes."

Paul says nothing, detecting sarcasm through the blur of his anxiety.

"It will be good for Dominique too," Bénédicte pursues.

"Tu en es sûre?" asks Dominique.

"Je l'espère."

They walk on, down an ancient Surrey lane, which, on a superficial level, is timeless. Tucked behind its high hedgerows and their depleted biodiversity, Surrey's discreetly wealthy hope they are insulated against unwelcome change. The lane meets a road, which is a relative upstart. As the village's thoroughfare, it used to have a village shop. Now, in theory, it has a chapel and a pub, but both are locked and as silent as the ruins of a more ancient chapel in a nearby field where the only worshippers are sheep whose god is grass.

The Bartholomews live in a meander of houses carved out from farmland in the 1990s. It doubled the size of the village after the quashing of vociferous local opposition, which was led by Rowena. Her pleas for wildlife were no match for the developers' dream of profits or for the aligned interests of the local planners. The scale is all wrong and the Surrey hung tiles that would supposedly render them "in keeping" are insufficient in quality and quantity. Bart and his family are at number 6, eager to receive their guests and usher them speedily into the back garden, which feels far too small for the size of the house and barely big enough for the requisite socially-distanced contact. Paul hands over a bottle of champagne and Bénédicte presents Agnieszka with a box of the best chocolates a supermarket can provide, while Dominique, Poppy and Daisy awkwardly make each other's acquaintance.

"It's strange we haven't all met before" says Bart. "It feels overdue."

"We just needed a plague to make it happen," says Bénédicte without a hint of a smile, suddenly aware that she never really liked social occasions even in less edgy times. As far as she was concerned, the only compelling reason to go to a party was to find your man, which supposedly she has done. She doesn't have Polly's drive to squeeze a story out of everyone she meets or Paul's blokey networking skills that belie or compensate for his tiny number of friends. Then again, could she have borne staying behind with Rowena?

"In any case, it definitely calls for champagne," declares Agnieszka, ordering Poppy to fetch some glasses.

"I hope you're all keeping well," says Bénédicte, an enquiry based as much on self-preservation as concern.

"We're doing our best," says Agnieszka. "I used to regret we were stuck out here, not in London, but I think we're healthier for it. I worry for the girls though. They should be at school."

"It's family bonding time," says in Bart.

"I'm glad to hear you say that," says his wife, chipping at the social veneer.

"I mean it, darling," he says. "In principle."

"We've been bonding with Paul's mother," says Bénédicte. "But we needed an afternoon off, didn't we *mon amour?*" she says with a glance at Paul, who is still too jumpy to rise to the bait.

Agnieszka spies Poppy emerging with the glasses and gets to work on lubricating her prickly guests and her evasive husband. She shares with Dominique the sense that Surrey has codes that will be forever alien to anyone born anywhere else.

Poppy, Daisy and Dominique are handed shot-size glasses of champagne. Dominique feels short-changed. Her Cognac grandparents would see no harm in handing her a brimming flute that would send her into a pleasant haze of carefreeness.

"How do you like Surrey?" asks Poppy, who has inherited her mother's concern for polishing the social surface.

"I'm not sure," says Dominique. "I'd like to go to London."

"London's much more fun," says Daisy, sipping uncertainly at the poison in her shot glass.

"But not at the moment," says Poppy from her older, wiser vantage point. "Everywhere is closed and empty. We have more to do here. Everyone in London is trying to escape."

"What have you been doing here?" asks Dominique.

"The best thing has been horse-riding," says Poppy. "I always wanted to, but I could never get home from school in time. Now I can. You should come along."

Dominique says nothing. She's tortured and terrified. She's being asked to do the thing she most wants to do that her mother forbids.

"Do you ride too, Daisy?" she asks, to deflect Poppy.

"I'm too young," says Daisy.

"That's not true," says Dominique. "You're only a year younger than I am."

"But the horses are too big."

"Then you need a pony."

"You sound as if you know about horses," chips in Poppy.

"My family does," says Dominique. "I don't really and dad prefers bikes. He says they're easier to control than horses, though he once had a serious fall. He doesn't like to talk about it, but sometimes he still has a slight limp."

She feels she's giving too much away in her desperation to change the topic of conversation and because she's so unused to other people she no longer has any idea what should or should not be said. Daisy, who clearly has no such concerns, leaps to the rescue.

"Our dads have been friends for ever," she says.

"She means since school," says Poppy, in patronising big-sister mode.

"Yes, they went to one of your English public schools," mutters Dominique, thinking of how much her mother disapproves and maybe even her father too. Until now, she had been happily making her way through the French system.

"You don't have them in France?" asks Poppy, though she's pretty sure the answer is no.

"We don't. We like to think we don't have a class system," says Dominique, suddenly aware that English class begins in the classroom. She's pleased with the thought even though she dislikes the reality.

"Because of your revolution," says Poppy, who has been brought up to believe England would never do anything so violent, at least not collectively and overtly.

"England probably needs one. Maybe it is even getting one now," says Dominique, wishing the adults or Daisy would step in to sustain the conversation. She likes Daisy for the same reason as she likes Jack: she has yet to learn social deceit.

As if reading Dominique's mind, Agnieszka materialises with plates and serviettes and tells them to come along and tuck in.

"Yippee," says Daisy.

The posh picnic fare is very different from Rowena's

meal for one at her kitchen table. She is surprised to find herself glad to be alone with a lunch of bacon and eggs – one of her guilty pleasures that she has denied herself in the presence of Bénédicte. If only Paul had married that nice, manageable girl who used to live in the next cottage, but then Rowena loves Dominique for the attitude that she considers stems from her genes.

The old neighbours have long since moved and been replaced by a new generation. Rowena has failed to find any connection. There has been little need. The plots adjoin but the houses are detached and distant from each other. The only contact has been strictly business-like exchanges about overhanging branches and replacement fence panels and recently, a note apologising for the noise as a tree surgeon is coming to chop down "the old pine tree". Rowena ached to object. She loves that tree that has been part of her horizon for decades, but she was forced to agree with her son that the battle is lost. The tree is not protected, many of its branches are dead, the neighbours can argue with reason it is dangerous and the local council, even if it could be persuaded to take the side of nature, is too busy dealing with its own survival. The timing is surprising, though: VE Day in lockdown. Rowena supposes the bill will be discounted and settled in cash. In any case, only a minority seems to be paying any tax in the distorted economics of lockdown. She takes up her phone and heads into the garden to take one last, heart-broken shot of the pine that stands between her and downland hills. If she can work out the technology, she plans to expose the tree-killers online.

No sooner has she captured her pine than a dirty white truck has drawn up, two men have disembarked and lugged a portable chainsaw towards the doomed tree. Within minutes, its nerve-shattering whirr has filled the air with the exhilarating smell of pine; a final gift to heighten the overwhelming sense of sorrow at nature's pain. Rowena dashes out with her phone again and accidentally presses the video button. She doesn't know it but she has recorded not just the sound but the sight of Fischer, the former tree hugger turned tree feller, stripped to the waist, wearing a harness and shinning up the trunk to saw off branches before the whole thing will be brought crashing to the ground.

15

For Tante Simone, as Bénédicte has always called her, May 8 is the day when even more than any other she thinks of her daughter Jeanne-Hélène. It was cruelly fitting that someone defeated by life should have died on a day that for her compatriots stood for victory. The marriage of her beloved cousin François, Tante Simone's true nephew, had been the final blow. Jeanne-Hélène could no longer sustain the deluded hope that, like a parasitic creeper, kept her upright but decreasingly alive. The institution where she had lived accepted that Jeanne-Hélène had been punished enough for a crime that was Fischer's, not hers, and released her to the care of her mother for a few final months. The death certificate said heart failure followed by a long list of underlying causes.

Tante Simone has since lived on aimlessly. She thinks she is indifferent to society, and yet cannot deny she is cheered by a neighbourly visit from Claudine. Claudine cannot believe that lockdown could possibly apply to people who have been nowhere and seen no-one. Moreover, she has also told herself Simone cannot be left alone on an anniversary that for her represents only personal battles. She lets herself in through the rarely-locked French doors that lead from the neglected garden to Simone's kitchen. As she expected, Simone is sitting at the table with a pot of linden infusion before her. It's the table that has witnessed so much. The table around which Simone and Claudine have shared their respective tragedies and that once bore a pot of poisoned *tisane* that Simone might have drunk had not Claudine walked in. Today the *tisane* is harmless, mildly health-giving, and Simone reaches for another cup from her kitchen dresser.

"I brought you a present," says Claudine, placing a bottle of her husband's *pineau des Charentes* on the table. She knows Simone prefers the sweet *apéritif* made with grape juice and young *eau-de-vie* to Cognac, the heavier *digestif*.

"That's very kind," says Simone, kissing Claudine twice on each cheek in defiance of all the government strictures to avoid spreading the pandemic.

"Are you okay?" asks Claudine.

"Are you?" asks Simone. "I lost a daughter who had nothing left to lose. You lost a daughter who had much to live for."

Claudine's *oui* in response is barely more than an exhalation.

Both fall silent. So much to say and yet nothing that could make any difference.

"How is Dominique getting on in England?" asks Simone after a sip of *tisane*.

"My daughter's homesick. For Dominique, it's an adventure, but of course I worry. I've never really liked Paul's mother."

There. She's said it.

"Oh really?" asks Simone, her interest slightly piqued by the dropping of the social guard; the avowal that Claudine, with her married daughter and grand-daughter, is not so much better off than the multiply-bereaved Simone.

"Well, to be really honest, I've never really liked Paul either. He particularly doesn't get on with Jean. You know Jean, he doesn't say much, but he's hurt. He'd hoped Paul and Bénédicte would take on the vineyard, but Paul isn't the type. He doesn't think the vines have a future anyway and we should all just find something else to do with our lives."

"Olivier wasn't the type either," Simone says so quietly it's barely audible. She thinks of him almost as often as she thinks of Jeanne-Hélène. For Jeanne-Hélène, she feels tenderness and sorrow. For Olivier, she still feels anger, still raw and embittered by the completeness of his rejection. Jeanne-Hélène was the craved-for daughter who was meant to heal the pain that went before; a miracle child after her elder sibling was stillborn. But Jeanne-

Hélène was brain-damaged at birth by a rare mixing of blood groups. It served to confirm Olivier's superstition the incompatibility was his. He should never have settled in Cognac for a life alien to a Parisian intellectual. In an act he probably convinced himself was merely logical and the local gossips regarded as supremely selfish, he hanged himself, leaving Simone alone to bring up Jeanne-Hélène.

"He might have found peace in these times," Simone muses. "He would have liked the simple focus. It would have given him more time for the life of the mind that was all he really wanted. Everything else was in the way. I don't think children of any kind would have really suited him."

Her words are the distillation of years. She cannot know, but she cannot break the habit of extrapolating. She has developed her own version of Olivier; in her mind he is alive and evolving.

16

Paul could probably find a few derivatives to trade on the volatile, exhausting emotions that erupt from the irrepressible hope that programmes Polly to keep trying when she is fully aware she ultimately will fail. Reem, in her own way as calculating, seizes on the idea that Polly floated tentatively of a conference call with Bénédicte. She knows neither Polly nor Bénédicte has any stamina to tackle the simplest of instructions, so she promises she'll take care of the technology. All they'll have to do is click on a link. She sends it round, together with the announcement of a day and a time based on the assumption that neither Polly nor Bénédicte will muster the energy to object and only she is being forced to be awake at an unusual hour.

Bénédicte's challenge, as everyone sneaks around Rowena's house, acutely aware of each other, is to find any time to take a call when she won't attract attention. With attention, comes criticism, given Rowena's puritanical disapproval of all activities that are not gardening, plain English cooking or housework, unless of course she is involved and they somehow allow her to reinforce her sense that she can perform them more expertly than the stupid mass of humanity.

Under her sway, the days have settled into a routine broken only by the attempted May 8 celebrations that left them as unrelaxed as it is possible to be, as if in punishment of their foolish craving for warmth and satisfaction. Bénédicte had almost physically itched with the sensation the virus was everywhere as she watched Dominique getting far too near to Poppy and Daisy. Her instinct was that Poppy, a bit too grown-up and yet not, could be a dangerous influence. Somehow, English youths seem more wilfully independent than their French counterparts, she thinks, perhaps because their parents are too conservative. Of course, her parents are conservative, as Paul has told her so many times, but they're not obsessed with power and control. She'd also overheard some of the horse-riding discussion and has braced herself for an argument that has yet to happen. That it hasn't has only added to the nervous sense of latency. She's sure it will.

They'd arrived home or wherever they are to find Rowena had managed to record a video of Thomas Fischer in the neighbours' garden wielding a chainsaw. "Good God, it's him," Paul had exploded. "Are you sure?" Bénédicte asked, registering the alarm on Rowena's face, as well as on Paul's.

He is sure and soon he has convinced everyone else there can be no mistake. Rowena insists on calling the police to inform them that a dangerous criminal, who should be rotting in a Saudi jail, is felling trees in Surrey and she has video proof. They ask her to send the video by email, but even she cannot dispel the impression she is being fobbed off. Everyone and every service is in survival mode. The police will pay attention when Fischer becomes a hot, not a cold case.

For Bénédicte, the benefit of the nervous disruption is that Paul and his mother take to spending hours strategising against the shared enemy. It becomes a pastime and a bonding exercise that entails conversations filled with family references Bénédicte has no desire to follow. If Rowena is to be believed, Paul's holidays from school were the time for getting into scrapes with the locals that forced her to intervene. It was as if the rigour of school had only served to compress the problem of adolescent anarchic energy into a six-week campaign of terrorising the neighbourhood, although nothing Rowena recounts is so very bad. He'd scrumped apples from the vicar's garden, even though their own garden had a stock of its own, and he'd fallen into the disreputable company of Vernon. Vernon was the kind of lad who would have grown up to be a tree feller, though neither of them is sure whether he got as far as growing up. What Paul had ever seen in his company is a mystery to his mother, who fails to recognise his need for a foil. She chatters on inconsequentially, as if cosy reminiscence can insulate them from their present dangers. They luxuriate in all sorts of scenarios and launch a joint offensive on the previously shunned neighbours, who are questioned remorselessly about their choice of workmen. Eventually, they hand over a phone number that just rings and rings.

Bénédicte leaves Paul and his mother furiously disputing its accuracy, while Dominique is in her room supposedly tackling schoolwork. Bénédicte slips away, heart-pounding, to click on Reem's link.

It's another limpid morning. The sky is unbroken blue. Birdsong is either louder or just seems to be as the background drone of aircraft and cars has become quieter. Bénédicte finds herself taking a bridle path into woodland. She smells that horses have passed through before she notices their prints and again wonders how long she can avoid confrontation with Dominique. She strides on, registering the last of the bluebells that reached an early peak in April, when she was told, by Rowena, they used to be one of Surrey's marvels but then the Spanish bluebells came to outnumber the more delicate English ones. The idea that the Spanish ones could, in nature's terms, be superior was lost on the teller.

Just before the appointed hour, Bénédicte finds a clearing that will have to serve. She perches on a tree stump and takes out her iPad, marvelling at the strangeness of being alive, here, now in this corner of the universe and being brought together with Reem and Polly by a magical device that in the space of a decade has become omnipresent. She feels she's a character in a modern fairy tale, lost in the wood and facing, at best, an ambiguous ending.

"Hello, hello," chorus Reem and Polly, competing with the birds.

"Hello!" says Bénédicte, suddenly nervous she'll be overheard.

"Where are you?" Reem gets her question in first.

"I'm in…" Bénédicte and Polly begin together.

"You first," says Bénédicte.

"South London," says Polly.

"Surrey," says Bénédicte. "I'm in a wood."

"Why?" asks Reem.

"Somewhere to hide," says Bénédicte. "Where are you?"

"I'm in California," says Reem. "I got a university placement here."

"Congratulations," they chorus.

"You're still working on green energy?" asks Polly.

"Yes," says Reem.

"How's lockdown in California?" asks Bénédicte.

"Can't complain," says Reem. "I can see the mountains and I can drive to the sea."

"Sounds fabulous," says Bénédicte. "It's beautiful here in a gentle way, but it feels like punishment. We've all spent far too much time running around and now the music has stopped and we just have to keep still wherever we happen to be."

"I know you're not meant to admit it, but I love it," says Polly. "I feel as if before I spent so much time trying to be something I wasn't, waking up in strange hotel rooms all over the world and constantly feeling sick with nervousness that any story I could concoct would never justify the travel budget. I was part of some ridiculous game when I didn't understand the rules. Now I just process other people's words in my sitting room. It's a relief."

Her friends fall silent and Polly feels she needs to add caveats and apologies.

"Of course," she says. "I know I'm lucky. I got so much out of my system, out of the system. And I know the economy is melting, young people are pent up and desperate to have fun and old people are lonely and dying."

"It's not just the old. My husband has died of it," Reem states as coolly as if she were reporting the loss of a family pet. Bénédicte and Polly are profuse in their concern, but Bénédicte can't suppress the hunch Reem is lying. Whereas Polly's striving for the truth can amount to a shortage of survival skills, Reem has always been maddeningly hard to read. She probably wouldn't hesitate to lie for the sake of a psychological experiment. Bénédicte struggles to believe she could have been married and been made a widow without until now saying a word. It's almost convenient; she has found an opportunity to at once create and destroy the private life whose apparent absence was an endless source of speculation for her international friends.

"Do you want to talk about it?" asks Bénédicte. Judging by her own experience, she would not want to say a word.

"There's not much to say," says Reem. "It was an arranged marriage. We didn't know each other very well."

There's another pause, as Bénédicte wonders if it is the simple truth after all.

"You're still married to Paul?" Reem asks.

"He's why we're here, staying with his delightful mother."

"And you Polly?" asks Reem in what is tantamount to cruelty, Bénédicte thinks. She's sure it's a sore point for Polly.

"Oh, I'm just hopelessly single," says Polly, affecting a laugh and wishing the conversation had a formal agenda. It is entirely dissatisfying to organise a conference call just to shoot the breeze. For all her protestations of no longer having fire in her belly, she starts straining for a story.

"Didn't you say Paul had seen Fischer?" she asks.

"I did," said Bénédicte. "I thought he might have been imagining it, but his mother managed to take a video of him sawing down the neighbours' tree. Now he's vanished into thin air and they're obsessed with trying to track him down. They spend hours plotting together."

"Wow," says Polly. "That is a bit scary. How did he get out of Saudi?"

"He was barely even there," Reem offers. "They did some

kind of deal. He must have had something on someone."

"But what on earth is he doing in Surrey?"

"Well, last time round he was after Paul," says Reem. "And now he's probably sufficiently bored to pursue a grudge."

"We could give ourselves a lockdown project too," ventures Polly.

"Get him caught, you mean," says Reem.

"Well, isn't it worth a shot?" asks Polly.

"Paul and his mother are giving it their all," says Bénédicte.

"When did they see him?" asks Reem.

"Last week, assuming they really did. He could be anywhere by now and the police don't care. They're too busy enforcing lockdown and witnesses are thin on the ground at the moment."

Briefly, they all pause. They've almost been here before in what was another life, when they could meet in an elegant hotel and hatch their plans for outwitting an international criminal over afternoon tea. With so much failure behind them, it is harder to believe in any cause and with death stalking as tangibly as in medieval times, it seems imperative to choose a cause that is worthwhile.

The conversation meanders on. Polly talks about the overheard conversations on the common. She finds herself explaining that common as a word has become devalued, but it has great beauty, especially in these times of exaggerated individuality and solitude. A common is a shared place and a place for sharing. She hopes her common, which of course is not hers, will yield material for a book. "Common conversations," with a subtitle "overheard in a time of plague". Bénédicte and Reem promise they would buy it. Bénédicte even sounds sincere. She says she needs a summary of the *Zeitgeist* that is more coherent than Twitter. She's warming to the subject when Reem declares she must go. She has an incoming call. "The host has ended the meeting," Bénédicte's iPad informs her. Without the long goodbye of any Cognac encounter, she is thrown back abruptly to her solitary self and suddenly, uncomfortably aware the stump she is sitting on has been recently sawn. It could have only been her anxiety to press Reem's link that prevented her noticing before.

17

Fishing for Fischer is for Polly just another addition to the lists and future projects that dominate her days, while her nights are shot through with dreams of the foreign destinations, commutes to the office and the colleagues who have slipped from her grasp and that in the conscious daylight hours she tells herself she does not miss.

She's also wondering whether "Common conversations" could go global: snippets from the around the world as humanity confronts a common enemy but/and fails to agree on a common strategy as the usual vested interests seize the opportunity to advance their own agendas. She knows she's dreaming. In any case, the most interesting conversations take place behind closed doors. Especially now the virtual world and its overwhelming possibilities are in the ascendant, she should be hacking into the dark web, not eavesdropping.

Dominique who tends to accept online possibilities are

as any other, wouldn't disagree with the view that

.body is out there in the ether is thinking the same

.nmon thoughts as someone else at any moment, past or

resent.

She is processing her literature lessons and thinks she might have at least one *Doppelgänger*, which is another of the concepts her literature teacher has taught. Madame Bellebeau is the one teacher Dominique misses because she ignores the rules and dares to stretch her pupils beyond their years. Her lessons sizzle with unpredictable energy. It's as if she relishes what all the other teachers do their best to suppress.

In the *Doppelgänger* lesson, the most unashamedly precocious girl in the class, straining to impress, demanded to know whether there was such a thing as a *Gegenübergänger* or precise opposite, physically and mentally. "Wouldn't that be more interesting?" she asked. "I think it would be even harder to identify," Madame Bellebeau replied calmly. "And to an extent, it would be missing the point. Our identity is far more threatened by an identical, or nearly identical rival than by an opposite. Even if it's an entirely imagined rival, as we've just seen in that short story we've just read, the terror is real and it shatters the sense of self."

Dominique's rival is the other Dominique and all her mother's efforts are channelled into ensuring she is not identical. Now Poppy is taunting her with horse-riding and she's tempted and terrified in equal measure; terrified not just because history can repeat itself but in case it doesn't and she has no talent; tempted because she is desperate to be physically on the move.

She takes up her literature assignment from the one teacher she doesn't want to let down. Madame hasn't given up on *Doppelgänger*s, but now she is giving them a happy ending. She has turned to her beloved Shakespeare "her first and purest love," as she likes to tell her students, risking an adult-like joke. Only Shakespeare, she says, is universal because he is so infinitely open to interpretation. He's also universal because he encompasses everything essential and surely engendered the *Doppelgänger* concept, with his sets of twins and agonies of confusion until characters emerge comic and whole. At times, the audience must sit back and relish almost unbearable tension, while suppressing the urge to leap on to the stage and explain the misunderstandings because audiences, like wildlife photographers, observe from behind a lens; they do not intervene. The doubleness can also be much more subtle: the idea of a parallel life that echoes and informs another, implicit in the very idea of watching a play performed on a stage.

Mme Bellebeau requests a creative assignment on parallel reality. She suggests riffing off Shakespeare. She has no objection to her pupils simply consulting a plot summary. Equally, they can imagine what Shakespeare and his characters might have made of lockdown. After all, they knew all about plague. But she's too wise to insist. A non-Shakespearean assignment, provided it is well-written and imaginative, could also make the grade.

Dominique opens one of the diaries. It's the obvious thing to do. She has a parallel reality within a parallel reality. She thinks she can beat the class show-off with this.

She begins with the scene when Molly's mother is taken away in an ambulance that drives through streets strewn with the rubble of war. It's her final journey to an asylum she will never leave. Dominique tries to imagine the long, draughty ward with high ceilings, where patients are by turns quiet and listless or raging, day after day. They have no contact with anything external to change their internal hopelessness. They have no private possessions to anchor their drifting personalities. She borrows from one of Aunt Ida's diary entries "rational seems such a beautiful word in a mad world". She is wrestling with the French translation – *rationnel, ou bien sain?* seem too tame – when she hears a scream.

18

Bénédicte returns to a house in turmoil. Rowena is weeping and again demanding the police be called. Paul has made her tea and is asking whether she is sure her ring has been stolen. She says she is. She had removed it for cooking and put it in its pot on the windowsill, as she always does. "The window was open?" "Yes, it was." "It's possible a magpie took it," says Paul. "I'm sure it was a human thief," sobs Rowena. "I'm almost certain the lid was on the pot and now it isn't."

This is worrying. Paul does not think his mother is senile, but he knows trying to get the police on the case would be hopeless. First, the increasingly notorious Gray family has bothered them with wild tales of an escapee from Saudi justice and now they say a ring has been stolen, nothing else, just a ring.

"I'll take a look round the garden," he says, leaving Bénédicte alone with his mother, which she knows exposes

her to the risk of a lecture. They emerge fully formed as if Rowena stores them up in readiness for any even half suitable moment. Bénédicte somehow never has a ready retort, which is probably a good thing. She could only confirm her utter wrongness, just as her efforts to help are pointless because she does nothing Rowena's way.

"Do you want more tea?" Bénédicte asks, knowing the answer will be no, possibly with the added comment that the French don't know how to make it.

In the garden, Paul has found only Dominique who is marvelling at another day of blossom and birdsong and beauty at odds with the anxiety they are living through. However indifferent to humanity's plight, or even delighted by it, nature is providing consolation.

"Poor *grand-mère*," says Dominique. "That ring means so much to her."

"What has she been telling you?" asks Paul.

"About her mother and Ida and the jewellery factory in the war. It's almost as if she shouldn't have told me. She broke the spell."

"What do you mean?" asks Paul. "Has she been weaving you into her exaggerated memories? She sometimes gets a bit carried away with all that. It was difficult for everyone."

"But especially for her mother," ventures Dominique. "Her mother went crazy and her *grand amour* was killed."

"Even in that she wasn't alone," says Paul, who, like his father before him, is as eager to de-dramatise the family

history as Rowena is to dramatise it.

"But after all these years, it still would be really sad to lose the ring. She says it's flawless," says Dominique, relishing a newly-acquired piece of English vocabulary.

"Maybe," says Paul. He thinks the value of diamonds is particularly dubious. Without marketing, they are little more than pieces of glass, though the value of anything is a matter of negotiation.

He is staring at the iris bed beneath the still-open kitchen window. The irises are at their most spectacular. Over the years, his mother has exchanged her knobbly rhizomes, as Paul's father referred to them with a smirk, with the village's other garden enthusiasts. The result is a range of colours – wine-red, violet, mauve and yellow. He likes the pale mauve the least. The paleness seems to expose the oddity of their design, but it also alerts him to a straggle of human hair. It's very long and matted and brownish and it would be a perfect match for Fischer's unkempt lockdown look. It could have just blown there from the next-door garden when he was working on the pine, but then again…

He calls in through the kitchen window. "Do you have a bag or an envelope, or something? And a pair of rubber gloves?"

"Have you got some forensic evidence?" asks his mother excitedly, breaking off from a rather pointed enquiry of Bénédicte about her whereabouts at the time her ring disappeared.

"I'm not sure," says Paul. "It could be nothing."

19

Claudine has ventured to the shops. Even she has felt the urge for more human bustle than the vines, the roses and her *potager* provide. First, she headed into the centre of Cognac and found it shuttered and very nearly deserted. The only signs of life were at the café-cum-tabac in the main square that has managed to get itself an exemption, or perhaps just dares to carry on regardless, except any coffee, perhaps with a cognac, is snatched hastily at the bar and no-one is sitting around for sociable chat. She gets back into her ancient Renault and heads to the commercial centre on Cognac's outskirts. It lacked atmosphere at the best of times and now is the joyless arena where people, wearing masks, clutching lists and trusting no-one, push their shopping trolleys with the grim purposefulness of those living under a repressive regime.

The veneer has been stripped away. The hypermarket shelves have also lost their benevolent air of plenty and ease. Their stark, cheap functionality is glaring. There is no smiling saleswoman to offer samples of "the product of the week" and many lines have run out or are about to. Claudine sees herself beaten to the last bag of flour and realises the woman who has got there first is Madame Bellebeau, striking and unapologetic as ever, even in her mask: only she would have obtained one made from bottle-green velvet and secured with a flamboyant bow that highlights the waves of auburn hair that she attributes to Breton ancestry. Her detractors have other theories.

"*Bonjour* Madame Bellebeau," says Claudine.

"Madame Rivet!" exclaims the teacher, before embarking on an effusive flow of enquiries muffled by the density of her mask.

Claudine can feel the stares of the other shoppers boring into her with reproach: shopping can no longer be combined with idle chat. She suggests they meet in the carpark in ten minutes' time for a short, unmasked, at least in the literal sense, conversation in the safety of air that hasn't been recirculated thousands of times. She's almost embarrassed by her keenness. Social starvation is apparently as bad for the mind as lack of food is for the body.

They regroup by the trolley return point. Apart from the bag of flour, Madame Bellebeau has focused on luxury. She has chocolate, fine wine and truffle oil. She must have only taken the flour because it was the last bag, Claudine thinks bitterly. She cannot imagine her using it for any normal culinary purpose, though possibly as a prop in a drama production. She looks down ruefully at her cleaning products, coffee and the pungent cheese she needs to get home before it becomes unpleasantly ripe.

"How are you finding all this remote teaching?" asks Claudine, feeling somewhat out of her depth.

"Of course, I miss the children," Madame Bellebeau declares. "But your grand-daughter seems to be thriving. She has creative writing skills I had not imagined. It's so exciting seeing such talent, but such a responsibility," she sighs. "It takes all my effort to keep my students on the right track. They could so easily let all that potential go to waste."

"Oh?" says Claudine. She would be more pleased if the teacher were less surprised and if she didn't feel cheated that other people were enjoying more meaningful contact with baby Dominique, as she still privately calls her, than she is.

"What has she been writing?" she asks, beginning to regret her urge to be sociable.

"It's intriguing," says Madame Bellebeau. "I told the class to imagine parallel worlds and she has dreamt up an entire family living in war-time Britain, one of whom seems to be a full-blown schizophrenic, who really is locked down. It's the best composition in the class, but please don't tell any of the parents. You know how competitive they are. I was wondering where she could have got the inspiration. It's wise beyond her years."

"I've no idea," says Claudine, though she strongly suspects Rowena of providing some form of help.

They look at each other awkwardly and Claudine wishes she had not removed her mask. She would never have been able to hold her own with the confident Madame Bellebeau and her *agrégation* at the best of times. After weeks of peasant solitude, the challenge feels insurmountable. At least she's found a cure for her perceived need for society. In desperation, she declares she has used lockdown to reacquaint herself with Melville's *Le Cercle Rouge*.

"Oh, I love Melville," approves Madame Bellebeau. "I'm starting to see where Dominique may have drawn some inspiration from all that circularity and human failure to reform."

Claudine is pretty sure Madame Bellebeau is entirely wrong, but she lets it pass and says she must rush off to stow her cheese.

20

In a human mockery of energy conservation nature would abhor, Poppy and Daisy are bouncing on the trampoline largely ignored in "normal times", loved in lockdown and destructive of any artificial style their garden might attain. Daisy is desperately trying to jump higher than her sister and collapsing in giggles at her failure to do so. Daisy likes this collective detention. It means Poppy has less scope to run off and do whatever grown-up things she would rather be doing and more time for her younger sister. Poppy is ambivalent. Daisy, never attuned to what is important, is making too much noise for her to overhear the conversation between Bart and his friend Paul that has the air of being more intense than their usual blokey chat. Paul is staring intently at a pot of pansies Agnieszka planted in one of her efforts to blend in with the Surrey crowd and Bart has the air of a supplicant. After the honesty serum of several pints of beer, in the days when that was possible, Bart would have admitted that was how he tended to feel in the company of Paul. It makes no difference that Paul is the one living in a state of terror and theoretically seeking the support of his oldest friend. Just as nutritionists tell us the food you eat in your earliest years determines your health for all of your life, it's as if, early on, both established a way of relating and Paul had the luck or otherwise to engrain the habit of assuming the upper hand. Confirming his disadvantage, Bart, with the tactlessness of his younger daughter, has dismissed Paul's concerns about Fischer and shifted the conversation to his current obsession: shorting. Both know it is the riskiest of strategies. Both are sufficiently arrogant or reckless to think they can pull off what Wall Street's most cunning have failed to master and both are desperate to relieve the boredom. After all, humans are hard-wired to varying degrees to dodge and crave risk; too many precautions make them seek the kind of danger they think they can survive.

It's the instinct that made Dominique accept Poppy's invitation to go horse-riding. It was relatively easy to reply yes to a text about a distant-seeming prospect, but now Poppy has told her riding instructor and it is fast becoming a reality that she must either evade or confront. The first challenge is to get up sufficiently early and leave the house without the knowledge of her *grand-mère*, who wakes at dawn for tea and early gardening duties before the hours of the heat that characterise these preternatural times. Dominique reckons she just needs to get back by half past eight when everyone assembles for breakfast. She plans her route, carefully avoiding being within sight of the vegetable patch, and rehearses her explanation should she need one: a school project to record the sights and sounds of a summer morning. She's pleased with that. She might tackle it anyway now her desire to be a cool teenage rebel has been modified by her not-necessarily incompatible addiction to Mme Bellebeau's approval, though it's less stressful to be studious in lockdown when no-one can see whether you're being cool or not. And so, she steals out. It's already warm. She mentally notes for composition purposes how loudly the parent birds are singing, the insistent cheeping of their growing chicks and that the blackberries are well on the way to precocious ripeness.

In normal times, she would be virtually alone at this hour when anyone awake should be preparing for commutes to days in offices that have been exposed for the unhealthy waste of time they always were. Only power-hungry politicians could possibly miss them, her father says. She absorbs rather than articulates his set of views, formed by random experience and encounters, rather than careful reasoning, and neither clearly of the left nor of the right. Like his mother, he has shaped a self-justifying credo that he imposes on almost everyone around him. Dominique realises she knows so much less of her mother's opinions, except on the subject of horse-riding and *grand-mère's* cooking, both of which she thinks are best avoided.

The stables are part of a farm on the edge of the woodland where Bénédicte had sat on a newly-sawn stump. Dominique walks more slowly than her mother had, her pace slowed by guilt and nervousness, and when she reaches her destination, Poppy is already in the saddle, eager to be on the move.

"Hi Dom," says Poppy.

"Hi Pop," says Dominique, bridling at Poppy's abbreviation.

"Right," says Poppy, not quite oblivious to the edge in her new friend's voice. "They've got Bluebell ready for you," and she points with her crop to a stable door. Dominique is greeted with: "You must be Dominique. I'm Linda." Civilities over, she's fitted with the all-important hat, and helped onto Bluebell, another floral name. Bluebell is one of the smallest and gentlest of the horses, she's told, and off they go at a walking pace. Linda gives minimal instructions. Her main aim in life is the pursuit of her own enjoyment after her abortive attempt to soar through the dreary ranks of public relations ended in a severance package and she took up the offer of a friend to help at her stables. The instructions she gives Dominique are limited to: "Remember, Bluebell can tell where you're looking, so you need to focus on the way ahead. In general, it's a good idea."

Dominique dutifully stares at the path and grips the reins as they negotiate the roots and chalky unevenness, but her nervousness soon subsides. She relishes the height that allows her to see over the Surrey hedges and she breathes in the warmth and smell of Bluebell as she bends close to her when they pass under low-hanging branches. She wonders if she loves all this because it is forbidden or just because so many weeks of restraint have heightened her appreciation of what should be normality: closeness to another animal without fear.

Paul is also on the move. He has left Bénédicte lying in bed, sliding in and out of slumber while he cycles up and down Box Hill, almost able to believe he is still his teenage self, ambitious to get faster every day. Once he would have been infuriated that so many other people have had the same idea, but his dread of Fischer means he appreciates the safety in numbers. He also has an arrangement to meet Bart, who has arrived by sports car and awaits his friend with coffee and bacon rolls procured from a catering van run by an opportunist with a lower risk appetite and arguably, a better business model than Bart's and Paul's. Paul says as much.

"We could open up a rival bacon butty outfit. All organic, no nitrates for the discerning Surrey crowd," he says.

"Too much like hard work," says Bart. "And the margins are terrible."

They sit on the grass, Paul's bike safely beside them, and

look out at the Downs, stretching into the distance and eventually down to the sea and the Channel and France, thinks Paul. Bart is intent on the spreadsheet on his iPad. He acknowledges the view to the extent that he can't decide whether he would rather be in the bustle of the City. For him, it would be a more natural place to do business. Here, talk of trade feels unreal and that worries him. He tells himself he's being ridiculous, but he can no longer tell the difference between superstition, hunch and sound instinct.

21

Bénédicte has no sudden mother's instinct that Dominique has escaped, but she is aware Paul is no longer at her side. She could be worrying, not just that he is prey to Fischer and his own demons, but at his proximity to Bart and to the temptation for trading she considers no better than theft or, more precisely, fraud. Instead, she is struggling to find the motivation to even be anxious when, day after day, she wakes feeling as powerless and purposeless as a child. In psychological parlance, she has no agency. She thinks of women she considers have achieved more – Reem, Polly – and she thinks of her mother and Tante Simone, embittered by their fatalistic acceptance. She needs to act. She needs a project. Her mother would say she has Dominique; that she is entirely selfish not to pour all her energy into motherhood, but isn't it just as selfish to pass on the burden of failure and require the next generation to make up for your shortfalls or perpetuate a cycle of non-progress? She also has Paul. She can never change him, so should she cut her losses and leave him to his fate, or should she try to save him from his tormentor? She rehearses what she knows, just as Reem is trying to marshal her research material, as Polly has strained to identify the holes in her reporting and devise a strategy to circumvent the lies and paywalls that prevent her from plugging them, and as the Cognac detective Frédéric de Massol once pored over his lack of evidence against Fischer. Fischer's guilt eventually became *un acquis*. The problem is he is on the loose. He is preying on Paul and is possibly the thief of a diamond ring whose disappearance has shifted the atmosphere of the household from uneasy truce to hostile mistrust. Paul is above suspicion in his mother's eyes, but isn't it a coincidence Dominique had just learnt about the significance of *grand-mère*'s ring and then it disappears? "A coincidence but no more," Paul very nearly snapped at his mother. He is not so blinded by filial devotion that he cannot see the damage her insinuation has inflicted on the fragile household harmony. How could she even for a second suspect Dominique, who has no taste for old-fashioned jewellery and has inherited her mother's horror of practical jokes? And does his mother really think so little of the upbringing Dominique has received?

Bénédicte wasn't displeased to see Rowena fall short in her son's eyes, but she is not enjoying the sense that a storm is about to break. She toys with the idea of calling Polly, but it's far too early for that, so it will have to be her mother. The phone rings and rings. She imagines the bell of the decades-old phone, adjusted to the loudest setting, echoing around and trilling through open windows until eventually Claudine answers. She's slightly out of breath. She'd been tending her rose beds. "It's a pity her daughter and grand-daughter are not there to help," she says. Bénédicte dutifully agrees, although it's a task she considers particularly futile. She understands that her father cherishes roses as the early indicators of disease among his vines, but her mother's obsession with 100 labour-intensive rose bushes in beds that she insists must be weed, pest and disease-free has always struck her as masochistic. It's one of the many issues on which they differ. How little they have to say to each other is exposed without the helpful smokescreen of daily activities to relate. The danger is they might have to tackle fundamental issues. Bénédicte thinks through the events of the last few days for safe material while Claudine relates the great adventure of her shopping trip and encounter with Mme Bellebeau. And so Bénédicte learns from her mother how impressed her daughter's teacher is by her sudden blossoming.

"Is it so surprising that she can write?" asks Bénédicte, peeved that no-one seems to consider Dominique might have inherited her creative talents from a mother who devoted hours of her life to writing the publicity material for Cognac Cauvet until Jeanne-Hélène brought the company to its knees by throwing matches into its precious stores of eaux-de-vie.

"It's just that she isn't usually top of the class," says her mother defensively. "I'm sure she's very clever. I just wasn't sure she always applied herself. You were harder working."

"But less talented, I suppose," Bénédicte angles.

"I didn't say that."

"How's father?" Bénédicte asks, to change the subject.

"He misses you. Surely you can come home soon."

"I don't know. The rules keep changing. It's very hard to make plans. We feel we need to wait a bit longer."

"Couldn't you and Dominique come home and leave Paul with his mother?"

It's something Bénédicte has considered deeply. She doesn't rule it out, but she fears it would mark a definitive breach. It may be what he deserves, but she's not sure where it would leave her, quite apart from her reluctance to give Paul's mother the satisfaction.

"You would never have left father," she says.

"Perhaps I should have."

"You are joking?" she asks.

Her mother says nothing.

"I'm glad you didn't," says Bénédicte if only to fill the silence, as both sides marvel at what has just been said and wonder whether it's true. Putting it into words seems to have made it reality. For Bénédicte, who is only herself because her mother met her father, it borders on an existential threat.

"Are you there?" she asks.

"Yes. I was just thinking."

"What were you thinking?"

"We liked Paul at first."

"I suppose you liked father at first," says Bénédicte bitterly, regretting that the conversation has taken this dangerous path.

Again, her mother amazes her.

"I didn't like him at first. I grew to appreciate him and these days it hardly seems relevant."

"To think I rang you to cheer myself up," mutters Bénédicte, almost to herself.

"Well, I have something to at least divert you," says her mother, suddenly remembering how pleased she is with her latest Google search. "Though you might have seen it already."

"Seen what?"

"You host is in the newspaper again."

"Really?"

"Yes, the Darking Bugle or whatever it's called. She's appealing for the return of her solitaire diamond ring. She says it has great sentimental value and she's offering a reward, though she doesn't specify the amount."

"I don't see that working," says Bénédicte, mildly enough. Inwardly, she chafes that her mother knows more about those around her than she does.

Both sides utter a few platitudes before Claudine decides it's time to return to her roses. Bénédicte has none of the reassurance she sought. Claudine cannot decide whether she has eased or added to the burden of years of fiction – the glue that can hold families together until eventually it dries out.

22

"Where have you been?" Bénédicte asks, as Paul enters, sweaty in Lycra, as she puts her phone down on the bedside table. "Just the usual. Cycling up and down," he says.

"Why don't I believe you?"

"I've no idea."

"Well, maybe it's the truth on one level, but you've seen Bart."

"Would that be a crime?"

"Not in itself, if you kept your distance."

Paul peels off his designer cycling shorts and slides into bed. Bénédicte tries to push him out, unsuccessfully as Paul pushes back with double Bénédicte's force.

"You smell and we'll be late for breakfast," she protests.

"It won't take long," he says. "I'm overwhelmed with desire, *mon amour*," he wheedles.

Bénédicte's head tells her she should resist, but she finds

it's so easy not to and maybe it isn't too late for that longed-for second child to fill the void left by the first Dominique and all those miscarried children who refused to enter the world?

The second Dominique is showering energetically in an effort to remove all trace of the smell of Bluebell who delivered her safely back to the stables after a maiden ride that she considers has established her as the natural horsewoman she always knew she was. She even managed a trot. "Before you know it, you'll be jumping," Linda promised as she helped her dismount and wash down Bluebell.

Poppy hopes she was joking. Having fought off her younger sister, she's not keen to be upstaged by Dominique, whom she brought along to impress rather than be impressed by. That is the problem with friends: their ability to surprise you, although it was always apparent Dominique knew more than she was letting on about horses. Daisy has the grace to be almost entirely predictable. She rarely knows any more than she maintains, or even as much, Poppy ponders, as Dominique dashes off and leaves her alone with Dasher, her trusty steed. Poppy gives him a cooling wash and strides off to the barn in pursuit of fresh hay, on the cusp of rotting and yet sweet. That is a smell she likes. It's part of the whole early morning atmosphere as dust dances in the shafts of sunlight that penetrate the barn. Today, it is mingled with something far less pleasant: the complex, earthy, suffocating, almost decaying aroma of a human who has not washed for weeks. She nearly jumps out of her skin as she hears a cough, itself a terrifying harbinger of germs, and a long-haired tramp emerges from the hay loft and coughs his way towards her. She grabs an armful of hay and runs.

23

Breakfast is Rowena's preferred meal, especially in summer. She has done the first of her gardening tasks to whet her appetite and she can almost convince herself she is young again with so much all before her, including all those mistakes that this time around she would avoid as she relished the belief she had been born at mankind's acme and into a generation that was so much better off than each one before.

They're breakfasting outside, looking across to rolling downland and a view bereft of the neighbour's pine tree. The garden table is stacked with cereal, fresh grapefruit and then there will be toast. For Bénédicte, there is yoghurt and for Paul, his mother's home-made marmalade in a jar with a polka-dot lid and a hand-written, dated label. In the previous life of early commutes and a dash to school or the office, when breakfast was barely tasted, it would have seemed idyllic. Now the problem is finding an excuse to leave the table. Only Rowena, with her disinclination to progress to the parts of the day when she feels older and more tired, is truly adjusted to lingering over her English breakfast tea and toast. She has purpose enough in her garden, her cooking and her mothering and today she is happy, despite the lost ring, as her guests assemble, each harbouring the guilt of illicit pleasure. Rowena's happiness is innocent. This morning's visitor has been welcome: a hedgehog still up and about and snuffling for grubs when she watered her lettuces. Rowena marvelled at the narrowness of his – or her - myopic world view, sniffing the air, then nose to the ground with no aspirations beyond finding the next mouthful. As she marvelled, she got too close, prompting an angry hiss as he rolled into his defence-mechanism ball that is futile in the face of hungry badgers with sharp claws or of rapacious mankind and his cars.

She is expecting more visitors, as she announces to the amazement of all present: her nephew, son of her mother's brother Jack, who had been a moderately famous pianist until he died tragically early of a brain tumour. Her mother never got over that: she'd failed to protect her talented younger brother. She speaks without any apparent awareness of the parallel for Bénédicte, but Paul sees the need to move the conversation swiftly on. "I'd be glad to see him, but I thought we weren't allowing visitors," he says.

"He'll stay outside. It's a glorious day. We exchanged messages last night," his mother says, sporting her lockdown skills. "He's in the area for work. You know he's a photographer and has an assignment. He's bringing his son too. He said he was desperate for any kind of outing. Even the garden centre would have done, he said. It was his little jibe at me."

"An assignment near here?" asks Paul. "I thought he was a news photographer."

"I don't know what he's working on, but it might be one of those feature pieces he sometimes does. I expect he'll explain," says his mother with a firmness that brooks no questions as she pours herself a second cup of tea.

John duly explains to the wonder of Dominique and to, a lesser extent of Bénédicte, who considers her Cauvet days of choosing the most golden angle on a luxury product gave her a feeling for photography. His task is to capture quintessentially English countryside for an international audience. It's part of a grand series from around the world on the redemptive power of nature. Even his editors have had enough of bad news and are pandering to the human need for hope and reassurance. For the English contribution, they have lighted on Surrey as close to London and just about as English as it is possible to be. This is core England, not some blurred border region where the rules are unclear and the territory disputed. He has found village greens, thatched cottages, peacefully grazing sheep, crops almost ready for harvest and horses cantering through green fields surrounded by hedgerows.

Dominique orders herself to be calm. He could not possibly have seen her on Bluebell or surely, he would have said. She asks what the editors have chosen to represent Frenchness. Really, Paris is for her the heart of France and the Jardin de Luxembourg has lots of nature.

"That would have been a good idea," he says. "But I think they went for vineyards."

"Not in Cognac, I suppose," says Bénédicte.

"Burgundy. Nuits-Saint-Georges."

"St George has been claimed by England and is Burgundy truly French?" asks Paul, trawling through his brain for half-remembered history lessons.

"Of course," says Bénédicte.

"Yes, I know it is now, but historically, it was a separate kingdom, then the Franks came along. It was only part of France later."

"If you're being like that, Guillaume conquered Britain."

"But the Normans didn't stay," chips in Rowena.

"They remained in our language and they definitely entered the gene pool," says John. "We're all the same ultimately."

"Much as I love France and the French, especially Dominique," says Rowena, mindful of her son's warning she had overstepped a mark, "cultures are different."

"They overlap. Dominique is proof of that. You're half-English, aren't you?" says Paul, as if remembering mid-sentence that Dominique can speak for herself.

"Do you feel more French or English, Dominique?" John's son pipes up, throwing Dominique into a blush with a question so deliberately aimed at her. John's son is named Andrew, shortened to Andy, and Dominique is trying to resist the temptation to be fascinated by him and his cool father. They are talking about the refreshment nature brings, but for her, they deliver a taste of the great urban capital she longs to explore, where people are liberal and artistic, and cultures mingle and hang in solution rather than crystallise into odd structures.

"It depends," she says. "In France, I was always keen to explore Englishness, but I'm starting to want to be more French. I think your country is mad to leave the European Union." Dominique says that with far more force than she meant to.

"I think we're mad, too," says Andy. "If only I had been old enough to vote, I would have voted to stay, but for our government, it's about ideology."

Truly understanding a word is a mark of maturity. Some people never manage it, but Andy is getting there. He is beginning to appreciate what ideology means from the polemic he has read on social media that has become terrifying since people have been locked up at home incubating their toxic views.

Andy is sixteen, a year older than Poppy, thinks Dominique. She hopes Poppy and he do not meet. Of course, she doesn't really care. She's told herself it is only because of the diaries and lack of social contact that she is predisposed to be drawn to Andy and she doesn't need any messy relationship, but Dominique fears Poppy would manage to corrupt him, whatever that means, even though he seems thoughtful beyond his years.

Bénédicte senses electricity crackling in the air and forces herself to intervene in the conversation. With Paul as her principal guide, she still struggles to hold her own in an English debate, especially after so many weeks of barely speaking.

"I think Brexit is about protecting culture," she says. "There is a core of Englishness. Some people just want that. It makes them feel strong and important. French people understand that. They are very protective of their Frenchness, but I would say Frenchness is mostly about an entire country. Loyalties here can feel very local."

"What about Britanny, Corsica, the Basque region?" asks Paul.

"I said, mostly," says Bénédicte. "The exceptions that prove the rule, as you English love to say."

John senses tension too. He's thinking it is time to go, much as he finds himself relishing once again being part of any kind of debate, sitting around a garden table in this cottage garden that dear old Rowena has turned into a text-book study of Englishness. If it weren't very nearly dark, he would add it to his collection of visual clichés, leavened with ironic details that caught his eye, such as a gaggle of teenagers kicking a football around the village green that should have been the setting for a cricket match and that tramp with a ponytail and a smell that was enough to frighten the horses.

He stands up from the table and says they must be getting back. "I must love you and leave you," he says. "It's been a joy."

They all stand up, suppressing the urge for a farewell embrace. Even pre-pandemic, it was awkward when elderly ladies, starved of physical touch, planted their puckered lips, or the young and lusting wanted the social kiss to be so much more, but it also feels unnatural to part without touching. Bénédicte, in her unease, casts her eyes around the garden. All the talk of cultural identity has made her homesick. She almost thinks she is imagining things when she spots the hedgehog. She thought they were almost extinct in England.

"*Un hérisson!*" she exclaims.

"Oh yes," says Rowena. "The hedgehog. I saw him this morning. I put out some water. I think the heat is making him thirsty."

John picks up the camera that is always at the ready and is just in time to catch the moment when the hedgehog rises up on the surprising legs tucked beneath his or her prickly coat and hastens off through a gap in the hedgerow.

"I might have another image for my English nature series," he says.

"*Les hérissons* are very French too," says Bénédicte.

"Slightly different genetically, though," says Paul. "I don't think they've crossed the Channel much."

"*C'est de bonne guerre,*" whispers Dominique.

"What do you mean," asks Andy.

"I think you say it's fair enough," she says, not entirely sure that she hasn't shifted the meaning of the idiom from its essential form to her own private meaning. "I mean to be arguing whether hedgehogs are more English than French, or the other way round."

"We'll have to continue the conversation another time," he says with all the charm of a French youth.

"I hope so," says Dominique. "There's so much more to say."

Andy bumps her elbow with his in the permissible lockdown greeting that Dominique suddenly discovers can be more charged than the social kiss.

Andy's father is suddenly beside them and has a guiding arm around his son's shoulders, permissible contact Dominique finds she envies.

"Time to go," he says.

24

Dominique heads to the diaries, which have become a talisman. She just needs to check. Andy takes his name from Andrew, the dashing pilot who was Rowena's father and John is the son of Molly's brother Jack, whose piano practice gets repeated mentions. Sometimes, he played for hours, while Molly was torn between wonder at his talent and jealousy that she didn't have it. Sometimes, it was all too much, and she retreated to the attic, where she felt closer to her pilot in the skies. She would wrap herself in a 1920s coat that she found in a corner among all the other cast-offs from more frivolous times and read without the distraction of Satie or Beethoven or Bach.

To Dominique's surprise, Molly is haunted by Gide. She reads and reads *La Porte Etroite*, or *Strait is the Gate*, which Dominique will now have to order via the internet, even though she is convinced the class over-achiever will be reading Camus' *La Peste*, and any plague literature she can find in other languages. For Molly, Gide's portrayal of thwarted love and the painful suppression of desire, was one of the few books lying around in the house and that was how she discovered it. First, she read the English translation, which she learnt from a note on the flyleaf was a gift from her father to his cousin Ida, then she got hold of the original from a teacher at school and with difficulty read the French. While Jack stretched his hands around stirring, sensual chords on the piano three floors below in that tall, narrow house, Molly developed a fascination for the self-denial of Gide's heroine Alissa that was far more destructive than any requited passion and longed for her to give herself to Jerome, her cousin.

As Dominique pores over the patterns of the family history, Bénédicte makes her excuses and heads off to bed, leaving Paul and Rowena to clear the table.

"I'm glad they came," Rowena says.

"So am I," says Paul, dutifully but doubtfully. They've come to resemble the inhabitants of a primitive, island community, historically the norm and increasingly the norm again. Its rhythms are disrupted by the slightest outside contact and its subjects have no immunity to others' bacteria. An exchange of views that ought to be stimulating is an existential threat.

"Your father would have enjoyed this evening," Rowena says.

"I'm not sure he would have enjoyed lockdown, though,"

says Paul. "His retirement dream was to explore the world."

"He'd have adapted," his mother says with the confidence of someone most comfortable in her own culture who never really held with the restless motion that used to characterise society. She delighted in castigating it all as meaningless. Either it was businessmen avoiding proper work and pretending to be important or it was the masses thoughtlessly grabbing countries as the easiest way to feel they'd achieved something to boast about when all they were doing was behaving in the same way wherever they went, eyes blinkered to make sure their prejudices remained intact. She has been spared having to accompany her husband on the adventures that for him would have been truly exploratory in places where she felt only threatened and queasy and above all, lacking the illusion of control. She'd much rather be in her orderly house surrounded by chores that he found a pointless, repetitive waste of life – no sooner done than in need of being done again. For her, they are a comfort that provides the illusion of predictability to disguise the inevitable march of change and decay. They are her chosen drug.

As they stack the dishes, Paul, forced by Bénédicte to relinquish his refusal to be introspective, marvels at how, through action and reaction and marriage to a man who was almost her opposite, his mother became the person she is and produced him. He wonders whether he resembles her in any way.

While his relationship with his mother is that of a mostly obedient subject, his relationship with his wife is an ongoing war over a scrap of territory. Each wants to govern it their way and Bénédicte says his way is his mother's narrow, controlling way, shaped by her insecurity over a childhood she could have presented as a triumph over adversity. Instead, Rowena considers it was scarred by shame and has never conquered her inherited complexes.

The missing diamond ring was the sparkling treasure that emerged from those dark days and, as if by magic, it is back in its pot on the kitchen windowsill, whose lid has been left beside it to ensure they notice.

Rowena picks it up, her heart leaping, and rubs it against the window. It leaves no mark.

"Someone has substituted a fake and a bad one at that," she declares. "We'll find a letter demanding that reward, I don't doubt. They can't have it."

"Could it always have been fake?" asks Paul, almost giving away his prejudice that no diamond has worth.

"It could not," declares his mother. "I have the valuation certificate."

25

Polly has digested her pasta and pesto and has moved on to her notes by way of dessert. They are not satisfying fare. It would be so much easier to produce prize-winning copy if she were covering the big story, but isn't that part of what's wrong with this asymmetrical world? An elite, either through birth or cunning, derives power from the main events. A larger group of ambitious strivers temporarily thrusts its way into the outer orbit. For most people, the small stuff is their lives and is as important to them as the global headlines they barely believe because they are beyond their control. Even thinking about them is enough to feel powerless and therefore angry. They prefer to believe wild conspiracy theories closer to what they have somehow grown to believe should be the truth.

The butterfly trifles Polly has netted from wandering the common are mostly the vain worries and naive dreams of those excluded from information and influence. Anxiety runs highest over the calories consumed when the gym to burn them off is closed and over the grey roots revealed after weeks without a visit to a hairdresser. Office employees worry about the food they have left mouldering in office lockers they may never see again. They deliberate over whether to book foreign holidays even as they fight for refunds for the ones they have not been allowed to take. Most hope life will be "back to normal" by Christmas. Only a few admit that normal was never all that great, although whatever is ahead will be worse.

"If you think it's bad now, imagine in twenty years' time, when we're governed by a generation that's been home-schooled by badly-educated parents. What's more, they'll blame us for allowing this to happen," is one of Polly's better overhearings, as two people walked the dogs that lockdown society regards as almost as essential as children.

"I don't want to think about that," replied the fellow dog-walker. "I can't believe everything has gone wrong at once."

"It's generally the way," replies the wise cynic. "If you remove a card from the house of cards, the whole thing will probably collapse."

The other stand-out has been in French. French was once one of the more mundane languages that floated through the London air, but now all the visitors have dispersed, it's a rare treat. Polly doesn't hear enough to understand why this pair of speakers is away from home. Maybe, like

Bénédicte, they are held captive by relatives. From the conversation, it could also be because of work, a lingering excuse to roam in these virtual days, which manage to confuse increased globalisation with increased localisation, to be nowhere and anywhere. The woman speaker seems to work in fashion, the luxury end, and is seeking to sign a deal with an artist to create bespoke T-shirts, whom, frustratingly for Polly, she does not name.

They are arguing about the ethics. He says the artist is selling out. She says artists have always had to be pragmatic to survive and anything else is self-indulgence. Moreover, her label embodies the values of thoughtfulness and sustainability. It's a win-win for both sides.

"No such thing," he says. "And if you want to be really thoughtful and sustainable, you wear some of the trillions of rags already in circulation."

"You are in no position to criticise," she says. "You have spent your career financing the unsustainable. The most sustainable thing you could do would be to cease to exist."

Polly could not tell whether the glamorous speaker was in jest or earnest as they bickered their way around the common. She would have had to stalk them to know more. Apart from the danger of detection, that would break her own private rules that are based on an old-fashioned tenet she learnt as a cub reporter: if the top page is in public view, it's common property. Turning to the next page would involve trespass. It's a rule she has once broken, but to no avail.

26

What would have once been minor is major. What she would have been happy to disclose as the reason for days off school, Poppy was desperate to conceal. It was Daisy, of course, unable to deceive, who announced to the household that Poppy had a fever. The humiliating invasion of a test confirmed what she suspected and yet finds difficult to believe. Could it possibly be that that stinking, coughing tramp she has only fleetingly met has managed to infect her?

Poppy has had to share her news with all her contacts, as the authorities term them. That includes Dominique. Dominique in her own fever of anxiety called Poppy as soon as the alert pinged into her phone. She needed to be reassured that Poppy hadn't told her parents they'd been horse-riding together. That was always the deal. It was to be a secret. Secrecy was part of the thrill. Briefly, it was a bond, but suddenly, she does not trust her new friend, who has decided communication is to be one-way. Poppy texts to say she's too weak to talk and Dominique is left alone to wrestle with the dilemma of whether she can she risk infecting her vulnerable grandmother rather than increase the chance her mother will find out she has been horse riding with Poppy for apparently the first and last time. It should not be a dilemma: clearly her grandmother's health, life even, is more important than her mother's ire, but it feels more complex than that when she doesn't know whether there is a risk – that word again – or it could already be too late. Madame Bellebeau has taught her enough for her to see the irony that horse riding held a different danger from the one her mother had so feared. It corroborates that rule that forebodings and prophecies are nearly always too vague to have any use or meaning; as you seek to protect yourself against one threat, another steals up from behind. Dominique finds herself imagining a slight tickling in her throat and the ghost of a headache as she works on fabricating a story of having bumped into Poppy on a walk and the adrenaline courses as if she were in a competitive exam. She is aware the permanent edginess of the household has once again erupted into confrontation. She hears her parents' raised voices. She hates them to argue. The strain of suppression for her sake and Rowena's is palpable. She deduces her mother's doubts, her unhappiness at being here and her father's imposition of his will that might have led to disaster, it seems. They'd have been safer in rural

France. He has seen Bart who has seen Poppy and Paul has seen everyone and they've even had visitors who stayed for hours and lingered, unsuspecting, around the table. The relative freedom of long, summer days is over before they had appreciated how carefree they were. Another memory is darkened by a backward shadow. Suddenly, they must go nowhere and see no-one and the minutes feel like hours as they wait to discover whether anyone is ill and everyone is blaming Paul for being inconsiderate and thoughtless.

Dominique retreats to her room at the earliest opportunity. She needs to be alone with her guilt, the diaries and that terrible woodchip paper that reminds her of the kind of material she has seen gathering dirt and damp in crumbling properties in France. Why is it still there in this house where everything is "just so," as her grandmother likes to say? Dominique doesn't really believe the line that it's too difficult a job to remove it. She stands on the bed and starts to scratch away at it with her nails and immediately recoils at the feel. She must ask her father for help. Surely, he will agree it's the perfect task for these times.

But first, she picks up her phone and finds herself searching for Andrew on social media. She sends him a friend request. He replies almost instantly and asks her how she is. She's okay, she thinks, but they're all locked up – even more locked up than before. She doesn't have any symptoms, so she should be okay, but she hopes they are too.

"On va très bien," he replies.

"Tu parles français?"

"Un peu. Tu pourrais être mon professeur, ou bien professeuse, n'est-ce pas?"

They're both bored and it seems like an innocent, even worthwhile pursuit. They switch from texting to talking and the cousins removed are soon giggling at Andy's schoolboy errors and what seems to Dominique to be a hammed-up accent she can't resist imitating. His retaliation is to demand explanations of rules she barely understands herself.

"Je vois la logique que la peste est feminine," he teases. *"Mais pourquoi la voiture, et pas le?"*

"Soit feminine," corrects Dominique. *"Subjonctif."*

For Fischer, the rules of grammar and his effortless mastery of them have allowed him to communicate in all the world's main languages. He once could infiltrate any circle and become the agent of the most ruthless. Now, he works only for himself and lives on the peripheries where logic runs into exception and contradiction and the illusion of order gives way. He needs to understand rules above all to evade them for the ultimate freedom of an invisible, non-existence, unbound by any state.

A pandemic would be the dream if only he could control it and, virus-like, enter someone's life in an instant, invade their every organ and decide whether they will live or die. Instead, the ague has him in its grip. He is fighting to retain the grudge he has cultivated into a *raison d'être* to take revenge on Paul for having so much that he doesn't. Paul has slipped his grasp for a decade. His mother helped to land him in jail and for that, he is willing himself to complete what he started a decade ago. Armed with the portable chainsaw that suddenly seems so much heavier than before, he heads into the woods.

27

Bénédicte is Zooming with Polly and Reem, an activity she could not in a previous life have imagined herself doing. She has tucked herself away behind the elegant reproduction greenhouse, where Rowena hides her compost heap in a brick enclosure and watering cans and terracotta pots await their duties. One of the larger ones, turned upside down, is serving as a seat for Bénédicte. She has placed it next to a water butt that in previous years would have been full to the brim. Instead, weeks of drought mean it is almost empty of the rainwater Rowena reserves for her most sensitive plants. With the force of a physical pain, Bénédicte recalls her mother's *potager*. Rowena's garden lacks the authentic decay of the crumbling limestone walls and the early summer heat is a few degrees less intense, but the cloistered atmosphere of this hidden corner is the same. Were it not for the Zoom windows on her iPad, she could be in any moment in history – or rather in any of the forgotten pauses in between. She does not find comfort in the knowledge that whatever she experiences is entirely unimportant and will sooner rather than later be forgotten or misremembered, but Reem is upbeat.

"You have to believe everything matters," she says. "We all contribute a little, whether it's positive or negative."

"I suppose your research is going well," says Bénédicte. She realises she has been sarcastic without exactly meaning to be. It has become a habit. She hastily shifts the conversation to Polly.

"And Polly, how are your common conversations?"

"The least common was between two French people," says Polly. "I thought there might even be a story in it. I think she was a fashion designer and he was some sort of finance whizz. Talking of contributions, they were both accusing each other of destroying the planet. She was claiming the moral high ground, saying she wanted to commission an artist. Unfortunately, she didn't say who."

"What did they look like?" asks Bénédicte.

"Impossibly glamorous," says Polly. "She was quite willowy for a French person."

"Willowy?" questions Bénédicte.

"Tall and thin," says Polly. "Though it's true willows aren't that tall, but they are graceful and their slender branches sway in the slightest breeze. I think you call them *saules*?"

"*Oui, des saules,*" says Bénédicte. "But I don't think we use them to describe people. What about him? What kind of tree was he like?"

"Is this relevant?" asks Reem with an academic's desire to impose discipline on the conversation.

"It could be," says Polly. "Looks are part of who you are, how you think, what you say … whether we like it or not. And who you choose as you partner – if you choose anyone – is just as telling."

"Tell me about him," insists Bénédicte. She knows it's absurdly unlikely, but she is starting to believe Polly has seen Lottie with she supposes François in tow.

"The perfect complement – dark, serious-looking, designer glasses," says Polly.

"I'm sure I know them," says Bénédicte. "The world is small. I think I might have met someone you know, too."

"Oh?" enquires Polly, immediately thinking of Pierre for no good reason.

"He's called John and he's a photographer."

"That narrows it down," says Reem, her impatience mounting. She wants to get back to the excessively negative contributor she is desperate to stop.

"And he works for your news agency, Polly," says Bénédicte, again not exactly aiming to pointedly ignore Reem.

"It is a small world," says Polly. "There's only one John among the snappers that I know."

"Snappers?"

"Oh, it's agency speak. Photographers. They take snaps."

"He was snapping the Surrey countryside," says Bénédicte.

"Did he take any pictures of Fischer?" asks Reem, in a desperate attempt to force the conversation back to her obsession.

Even she feels the effort of staying focused on anything beyond the present moment when it's a struggle not to give into the feeling humanity is collectively dying and any future is only a dream. To Reem, it's the reverse of the years that felt like progress when her days were driven by agendas, travel plans and goals. She clings to the great negative of Fischer as she would cling to hope.

"I doubt it," says Bénédicte. "But I didn't even see his pictures. He was just trying to capture typical English life in lockdown for a feature. It wasn't his idea and I got the feeling he thought it was a bad one, but he was happy for an excuse to be in the countryside."

"I can look," says Polly. "You never know, though even if we have a rare photograph of an international criminal, will it actually help?"

"You never know," says Bénédicte. She is unable to focus beyond the terracotta pots. She cannot even make herself believe Fischer is a real problem or that she might be living in a plague house or that her husband's trading with Bart could be out of control – or that the supposed friends talking to her from a screen are more than a figment.

28

As he so often does, Paul has given into his daughter's insistence and is scratching away at the woodchip wallpaper that was the one reason he allowed himself to articulate for why he didn't smuggle girls into his bedroom during his teenage years when all his friends claimed they did little else. He feels he is unpicking the past that was at once a perfect, middle-class springboard for a fulfilled life – and yet was not. Otherwise, why would he have wasted it all on speculation – the very opposite of his parents' calm accrual of middle-class respectability, like a dense layer of moss? His modestly academic father and his doggedly gardening mother gave him every chance. He could have married the girl next door, followed his first instinct to become a doctor and cemented the family status as a pillar of the community. Even after he failed to do that, he could have been happy with Bénédicte, he tells himself, if only he hadn't allowed Bart to suck him into this ridiculous shorting that, unaccountably, is forcing them to pay out when there is no logical reason for stocks based on no inherent value to rise. He finds himself suspecting Fischer and tells himself that's irrational. It's just his guilty conscience playing tricks. Fischer surely couldn't know his trading positions well enough to whip up an army to trade against him, could he? As he wrestles with the sensation that Fischer has managed to enter his brain, he scrapes at the ceiling with an energy he didn't know he possessed.

It's almost as if Dominique is reading his thoughts and handing him a remote genetic excuse for his bad behaviour; he has simply come full circle.

"I was thinking about *grand-mère* and her Aunt Ida," she says. "She was a trader, like you."

"I suppose," says Paul. "But she never went short."

"What do you mean?" asks Dominique.

"Oh, just that she stuck to the fundamentals. I've been slightly more adventurous."

"She was very adventurous," said Dominique. "She went all the way to South Africa in the middle of a war. She stitched diamonds into her hems and her underwear. I can't even go home to France with nothing to declare."

"That rhymes," says Paul.

"I'm a poet and I don't know it," as *grand-mère* would say, says Dominique with only the slightest of smiles, the kind that from time to time flickers across the lips of Bénédicte and is the opposite of Daisy's unselfconscious peals.

"You don't feel here is home?" ask Paul tentatively.

"It's just so bizarre," says Dominique. "The times are bizarre and it's bizarre to be just permanently visiting *grand-mère* and then there are the weird things that keep happening and make everyone on edge. I want to go back to my old life."

"You can never go back," says Paul.

"Never to France?" asks Dominique, alarmed.

"I don't mean literally. I mean, nothing is ever the same again."

"And yet our teachers say *l'histoire comme une idiote se répète*," says Dominique.

"Well, that's true too. We repeat our own mistakes and we don't learn from others'. We get stuck in vicious circles and trapped by nostalgia. No one person can go back to how they once were. You can try to experience the same things again, but they will feel very different and probably worse. As individuals, we must always move on and as society, we should."

"You're not going to tell me again that Brexit is about false nostalgia and the Blitz spirit that never existed, are you?" asks Dominique.

"No. I'm over it. Sort of. If you ever recover from a bereavement, especially one that should have been avoided."

"But what about our house?" says Dominique. "It must be lonely without us."

"*Bonne-maman* is keeping an eye on it," says Paul. He doesn't admit his anxieties about his favourite bike.

They carry on scratching away at the ceiling, releasing decades of dust onto the dust sheets Rowena has draped around the room. She hadn't exactly welcomed the project. She said her mother had liked the paper. It was the need to please Dominique that prevailed. Rowena knew she could not risk offending her again after her not-very-veiled accusation of her only grand-daughter had prompted a rare role-reversal reprimand from her son.

"*Maman* wants to go back to France," says Dominique.

"None of us can go anywhere right now," says Paul. "Because I was stupid enough to see Bart."

Dominique could tell her father she had also been stupid enough to see Poppy and she doesn't exactly decide not to. She's confident he wouldn't tell her mother, but as with the diaries, she is waiting for her moment to confess. It seems so much easier, calmer, wiser to harbour secrets and guilt than to send them out into the world and discover the consequences. As far as she can tell, it's what people, families, societies do out of laziness and fear, or is it cowardice?

The scraping continues. Both are in their private worlds.

Both expend energy they would normally channel into a myriad daily tasks. Paul is the first to declare they need a break.

"Not yet," says Dominique. "I just want to do this really rough bit. It's as if the paper has peeled off and someone has stuck it back with extra glue."

"I'll help," says Paul, reaching into the corner with a force that makes a hole in the fragile plaster.

"*Zut*," says Dominique, suddenly echoing *bonne-maman*, not *grand-mère*.

Paul says nothing. He's reaching into the hole. He thinks he might have discovered why his grandmother liked the ugly wood chip paper.

29

For nature, it's another halcyon day and mankind, manic-kind, is trying to forget its self-inflicted cares in a frenzy of motion. People are walking, running, jogging, roller-skating and in Paul's case, cycling. Despite his ten days of inactivity, unless you count scraping a ceiling, he has recovered some of his old form. It's the good thing about cycling – stamina can improve with age. He could be glad to be alive, here, now, lost in the moment, if only he could stop thinking about how much Bart has made him lose and the impossibility of undoing a few acts of folly. Relieved from his plague anxiety, Bart has reverted to his default Tapleyism, the male version of Pollyanna syndrome that, strangely, is far more familiar to the masses. He wants to double down. "We'll get it back," he promises. "There are so many waves right now. We just need to find one to ride." But Paul at last is adamant. "I have to stop. I can't ask Bénédicte for money again. This has nearly broken us."

He hasn't told Bart he has a security. In any case, he has no idea of the worth of the rough diamond of many carats that he spent many nights of his life sleeping under. Such things are harder than most to price. There is no market as such and you need an expert to cut it, but would it have changed anything had they all known? Was it the fear that it would that made his grandmother leave it to chance to determine whether anyone would ever find it? She didn't want the responsibility of bequeathing a blessing that could become a curse? She has risen in his estimation for leaving such an intriguing legacy, though he can't understand why she didn't attempt to cash it in – or maybe she had tried and failed.

In the excitement of the find that promised a punishment amnesty, Dominique broke her silence and confided in her father about the diaries, diaries he had known about and never had the curiosity to read. He'd left them as undisturbed as the wood chip. Together, he and Dominique pored over the South African journey. The giant rough diamond was not mentioned. Paul asked his mother. She was mystified. Her mother had never said a word, but she had spent the final weeks of her life in Paul's room. Was Ida given it for a rainy day? Did she even steal it before she handed it on to the daughter who apparently decided to hide it? Maybe Molly had stolen it from Ida. Rowena hates to admit it, but she finds that idea plausible.

Paul cycles on up the incline and beneath the arches of

ancient Surrey woodland. Birds are singing, rabbits are hopping in the fields and deer are dashing for cover, living their lives in a state of constant strain as enemies lurk all around, ready to take advantage of the slightest lapse of attention. Paul thinks he is alive to danger – potholes hit at speed, cars, other cyclists overtaking and exhaling germs, but as he scours the road for perils, it never occurs to him a branch is about to crash down on him and that Fischer, weakened and wheezing and stinking will drag him behind a hedge. Every bone aches and Paul's quasi-happiness gives way to profound boredom with it all. The will, the energy ebbs and there is no reason for this formation of atoms to carry on holding together. It's the merest chance that it ever did. He has no illusions. Bénédicte will be free to return to France and she won't be paying for a bench with his name on to mark his favourite spot. Bart will curse that he has been left in the lurch by his trading partner, but only his mother will really care, he thinks. Even then, her concern will merely reflect the disruption of the natural order that dictates he should outlive her. He consoles himself he has given her a grand-daughter to improve on everyone who has gone before and whom he is heart-broken to leave behind. That – and a sharp kick from Fischer in his broken ribs – is all that prevents him resisting a slide into permanent unconsciousness.

"What more do you want?" asks Paul. "Can't you just leave me to die?"

"And waste my one chance to confront my nemesis?"

"Isn't that a bit melodramatic?" asks Paul, earning himself another kick as he thinks to himself it was his mother, not he that briefly ended Fischer's freedom to pursue anarchy. Through a fog of pain, he tries to think what he can possibly persuade Fischer to tell him, though what's the use if he's to carry it to the grave. Even if he survives his broken bones, Fischer must be highly contagious and is breathing with great difficulty all over him.

"What have you done with my mother's ring?" Paul asks, hating himself for sounding so plaintive.

"I gave it to Poppy, your friend's lovely daughter. I suppose you know she went riding with Dominique?"

Paul says nothing. It's so typical of Fischer to have been working on finding his next agent of evil. It's a reflex. It's what he does. It's how he is programmed. He can see why he would choose Poppy. Even Bart admits she has the devil in her. He says it with affection, but it's code for the dangerous combination of his wife's ruthless ambition and Bart's lapses of judgement. Innocent, giggly Daisy is far more likely to turn out well.

"I expect she'll give it back to help her father out, for a small fee."

Paul racks his delirious brain for anything Fischer might say about the murdered oil minister and the Cognac executives and who or what made him do it. There's an outside chance Fischer will tell the truth, according to the rule that people suddenly reveal all to people who are leaving, as agendas and strategies melt away, especially when they're leaving the world.

"Who did you kill? Castaniet? Furness?"

"They killed themselves."

"But you helped…. And the oil minister. Why did you do it?"

"Why not? The world doesn't need oil ministers."

"But what drove you?"

"How about rebellion from an overly-controlling mother? You should understand that. Yours is my next victim. All I need to do is promise I'll show her where her precious ring is and give a little cough, maybe a spit for good measure."

Paul should rise in fury with a final surge of energy. Instead, he receives a *coup de grâce* kick. He assumes he is seeing his life flash before him as the last people to dawn on his consciousness are Vernon, with whom he spent school holidays scrumping apples, and, with him, one of the women who rescued him last time he fell off a bike in Darking.

30

Polly is sitting on the common with Dominique and John and Andrew. For Bénédicte and Dominique, it's a farewell picnic. They are returning to Cognac. All around them people are relishing their new-found freedom and choosing to believe the plague has gone away, even though history tells us it is only waiting for its moment to pounce again. There is laughter; there are champagne corks and squealing children and adults. Polly has half an ear open for the verbal snapshots she cannot resist capturing, even if their fate will be to fester undeveloped in her notebooks. Should anyone listen to their little party, they might remark more silences than words. The group is so subdued an eavesdropper could suspect there has been a bereavement. There has not, at least not in the literal sense of the word. Paul was saved by his cycling helmet and the loyalty of a childhood friend and one of the angels of mercy who had found him lying on the ground once before. Paul has a bleary image of them fighting off his attacker and calling for an ambulance. Fischer vanished into the woodland, leaving only his chainsaw behind. The police have taken a cursory interest. The saw was covered in virus. That should be reason enough to track Fischer, rather than let him spread the plague over the countryside, Rowena attempted to insist, but the authorities seem to think it could be just as related to Paul as to an elusive fugitive.

Paul is recovering under the care of Linda's friend Sister Tanya Furness. Bénédicte and Dominique and Rowena have all been to the giddying brink of imagining life without the man who has been central to it. Bénédicte hates to give Rowena the satisfaction, but she is resolved to hand back the son it seems she only borrowed. She has bought her tickets to head to France with Dominique. After all, it's only natural she should want to spend time with her own family. There is no need to declare a formal separation, but Bénédicte is fast forming the view she's better off without a magnet for danger. To her, their little grouping of three never felt whole anyway, so does it matter if she breaks it up?

She is sitting next to Polly, who is next to John. Beside him are Andrew and Dominique. Dominique is enjoying her one and only outing to London, but instead of the edgy nightlife and anarchic fashion she had craved, they are in middle-class south London, home to the young and affluent and their designer children, the next generation, meant to have perfect skin and perfect teeth and perfect education to deal with the ravaged nature that is likely to be their inheritance.

Andrew's and Dominique's conversations have ranged widely during the high anxiety of the last weeks. His French has advanced as he has offered emotional support and they've shared the scraps they know about the family's diamond-dealing past. Now constrained by the adults around they have almost nothing to say.

Bénédicte uncharacteristically fills a silence with a social nicety. Perhaps months of Surrey lockdown have left their mark.

"I hope you'll all come to see us in Cognac," she says to no-one in particular.

"We'd love to," says Polly. "I need to revisit the scene of the crime."

"That makes it sound as if you did it," quips John and Bénédicte finds herself wondering if their rapport is more than professional or at least could be and why he hasn't brought his never-mentioned wife along.

"Well, as a species, we are collectively guilty," says Polly. "And we never really solved those murders."

"That wasn't your job, though," says John.

"No, but a real journalist should hold people to account when society doesn't."

"You're too idealistic," he says. "Journalists have less power than they ever did. They're as manipulated as the next person. I'm hoping Andy and Dominique will find something more sensible to do with their lives."

"But shouldn't we take up where you leave off?" asks Dominique. "I mean, it sometimes takes more than one generation. We shouldn't just give up."

"You have a point," says Polly. "I'd love to agree, but John might be right that I'm just misguided and, in any case, I haven't produced a next generation."

"You can still influence the next generation. My teachers influence me and they're not my parents."

"They influence you far more than your parents," says Bénédicte.

"*Pas du tout*," says Dominique. She means it. Suddenly she's thinking of her father and her eyes fill with tears. She dreamt of return to France, but not without the father she feels she can influence to the good and whose family is free of rival Dominiques. Another silence falls as by unspoken consent the assembled party is not talking about him today as he lies recovering under the watchful eye of Nurse Tanya Furness with frequent visits from Rowena.

The silence lets them all listen to the rest of the common and among the birdsong and the laughter and the dogs barking, they hear French.

"*Je le savais*," Bénédicte says to herself as she spots François and the willowy Lottie.

"You know them?" asks Polly.

"Not really," says Bénédicte. She is desperate not to

torture herself with the idea of what might have been and what some irrepressible part of her hopes still could be, but only because the unexplored avenues are always the most promising.

FIN

ABOUT THE AUTHOR

Barbara Lewis is a journalist whose career has taken her to London, Hong Kong, Paris, Brussels ... and Cognac. She read English at Jesus College, Oxford, before setting out as a trainee reporter on the Bromsgrove Messenger, where she covered anything from golden weddings to murder to the arts. A passion to explore the world beyond Britain led her to leave local journalism for international news agencies, currently Reuters. Another passion is theatre and she wrote a sell-out play for the Edinburgh Festival. Solitaire is the final novel of her Angels' Share trilogy.

Printed in Great Britain
by Amazon